Rules for Flying

Jacquelyn Johnson

©2020 Crimson Hill Books/Crimson Hill Products Inc.

All rights reserved. No part of this book, including words and illustrations may be copied, lent, excerpted or quoted except in very brief passages by a reviewer.

Cataloguing in Publication Data

Jacquelyn Johnson

Rules for Flying

Description: Crimson Hill Books trade hardcover edition | Nova Scotia, Canada

ISBN: 978-1-989595-48-0 (Hardcover - Ingram)

BISAC: YAF000000 Young Adult Fiction: General
YAF022000 Young Adult Fiction: Girls & Women
YAF058020 Young Adult Fiction: Social Themes – Bullying

THEMA: FXB – Narrative Theme: Coming of age
YXO -- Children's / Teenage personal & social issues: Bullying, violence, abuse & peer pressure
YXHB -- Children's / Teenage personal & social issues: Friends & friendship issues

Record available at https://www.bac-lac.gc.ca/eng/Pages/home.aspx

Front Cover Image: Cristina Zabolotnii

Book Design & Formatting: Jesse Johnson

Parts of this story formerly appeared in the novel Sam's Christmas published in 2019.

Crimson Hill Books
(a division of)
Crimson Hill Products Inc.
Wolfville, Nova Scotia
Canada

Crimson Hill
Books

It's a magical Christmas morning…

A winter storm means that Sam Park is about to get her biggest wish, to have a real family Christmas.

Trees are down. The power is out. But not even a storm can cancel Christmas for the Star family. There are gifts under the tree. Everyone sings carols. Soon, they'll gather for the big turkey dinner with all the trimmings.

To Sam, it's all wonderful. Magical. It fills her heart with joy.

Yet Sam also has a dark secret, one she can't possibly tell anyone, not even her two best friends.

Especially not them.

Even though this secret could ruin everything.

Then, all too soon, Christmas is over and Sam's worst fears are coming true…

Rules for Flying is a book about being true to yourself, standing up to your fears and following your heart's fondest desire.

For girls 10 to 13 who like stories about feisty girls facing real problems with courage and ingenuity as they discover their own voices and strengths.

Rules for Flying is the fourth book in the Morley Stories series of novels for middle school girls in grades 5 to 8.

Also In
The Morley Stories
Series:

Just Me. Morley

Feather's Girl

Sam's Gift

Rules for Flying

Find them all at
www.CrimsonHillBooks.com

Remember this always.

What you think, you are.

What you believe, you are.

But, most of all, what you do, you are.

Always think and believe and do your gift to the world.

Because you are the only one who can.

- Madame Boulanger

one

"Santa came! He was here! At our house! Santa really came! And there's a pink bicycle and I think it's for ME! Wake up, come on, wake up!"

I open one eye. It's barely light out. The room is cold. I want to snuggle into my sleeping bag and sleep some more. But Daisy isn't going to let that happen, for anyone.

"Come on! It's Christmas! He came! Santa came! And there's a bicycle! And it has a basket and streamers and everything! And it's pink!"

"Ok. Ok, Daisy. We're here." I hear Eira say. "Coffee first," Dom says hopefully. "Then presents."

But Daisy can't wait. Eira has swept back the living room curtains for the bit of light there is from the gray sky, revealing that overnight there was more snow. She turns a switch and the Christmas lights come on.

one

"And the power came back on!" Daisy squeals, until reminded that no, that's just the generator. The power is still out from the big storm. But the tree does look pretty, the most colourful thing in the room.

Then Dom is showing Daisy how to sit on her bike, Morley is helping Eira make hot drinks for everyone and Uncle Gus comes in with a plate of cinnamon toast he made with his new homemade toaster. Just something he put together this morning, he says. It's a sort of wire rack thing that you put bread in and hold over the fire, made out of old coat hangars.

Christmas morning breakfast, he says. His treat.

Then we're all opening gifts and saying, "Oh I love this!" and everyone's smiling. I figure there aren't going to be any gifts for me, so I go over to the piano and play some carols. Just because I feel like it.

But then Morley comes over to the piano with a gift wrapped in green tissue. "For you," she says.

It's a jade-green circle scarf. I know she made it. I put it on, feeling the kitten softness next to my neck. "Thank you," I say, hugging her. "It's perfect!"

Morley just about cries when she opens her gift from Eira and Dom. It's a laptop and it comes with a year of internet service, Dom says. "But what about Mom? She said no computers for kids…"

"We'll manage that when your mother gets home," Eira says. "Don't worry!"

Daisy can barely tear her eyes away from her new pink bike. But she does for long enough to open all her other gifts. There are a lot of them. She searches through the pile to find the ones from her dad, Danny. Because of the storm he couldn't get here for Christmas.

Gus gets a gift certificate to his favourite tool store and Dom gets a new e-book reader. And they both get scarves that Morley made.

Daisy loves the princess tiara her sister Morley made for her and puts it on right away. Eira's eyes light up when she sees it. "Morley – you designed this? It's fantastic!" Eira says.

"I know," Morley says. "It turned out even better than I thought it would."

Pixel and Feather get new toy mice with catnip inside, but they're both more interested in chasing each other through the piles of gift wrap until they collapse in a furry heap and fall asleep under the tree.

After all the gifts are opened, I nudge Morley, sitting next to me on the floor, and say to Daisy, "I think there might be some more gifts. In the tree!"

Daisy leaps up. "In the tree? Where?"

That's when she finds the red envelope for her. The one Morley and I put there last night.

Hidden among the branches are other envelopes. There's one each for Morley, Dom, Eira, and there's even one for me which is a suprise.

Daisy is so happy to get a letter from Santa, she doesn't even think about asking what the other surprises are, which is good because she already has opened just about all of them.

one

Eira's has two tickets for a skiing vacation to Whistler after Christmas. From Dom.

Morley's envelope has a gift certificate for her to pick out the phone she wants. She's thrilled. And I'm so happy, too, because now we can text, just like Jayden and I already do.

Dom just smiles and leans over to kiss Eira when he opens his. I never did find out what it said.

But I think mine is the very best gift of all. It's a card, with a house covered in snow on the front. The house looks like Morley's house, sort of. I know she drew it.

Here's what it says inside:

>Dear Sam,
>
>It's been so special to have you with us this Christmas. But it has been anything but normal, hasn't it, with the storm and so much going on?
>
>So this is an invitation to come and spend next Christmas with us, and your mother is also invited if she would like to come. Give us another chance to show you what a real Star Family Christmas is!
>
>Fondly,
>
>Eira, Dom, Morley, Daisy and Gus

There's a paw print under their names, which I guess is for Pixel and Feather.

"Thank you," I say. "I'd love to!" Even though I know it probably isn't ever going to happen. Not with us so far way away in Hawaii. That's where my mother wants us to move to.

Besides, I'm already having a real Star Family Christmas, the first and best Christmas of my life! And all because of that winter storm that started the night of Morley's sleep-over party.

When everyone is washed and dressed, we all have to go outside to see Daisy's gift to everyone. She made birdfeeders with Gus and used some of her birthday money to buy birdseed. Now the new feeders are hanging all around the front and back yards. At the feeders, chickadees zoom in, grab a seed and fly away, ignoring the blue jays who lecture any other bird who wants a snack. From a nearby branch, a male cardinal watches the feeders, waiting his turn.

Later, I get out my phone and find out I don't have much charge left. There's a message from my Tia Margaret and a picture of her with her own kids. There's also one from Jayden with more Tippy pictures. Tippy's my puppy but he's having a doggy vacation at my friend Jayden's over the holidays. In the pics, Tippy's got a Santa hat on his head and a new chew toy. He looks pretty happy.

Morleys' new phone isn't charged yet because the electricity is still off from the storm. Her Aunt Eira's phone is totally flat because Daisy was playing Candy Crush on it. Dom forgot to charge his before the power went out, so it isn't working, either. Morley uses mine to send a Merry Christmas message to her mother and her new baby sister Lily. They're still at

one

Kentville Hospital because Lily was just born.

Her mum and Danny, that's Lily's and Daisy's father, have agreed that, for a special Christmas sister gift, Morley and Daisy are each allowed to pick a middle name for Lily.

"How about Mary?" I ask. "Mary was the very first Christmas mother."

"Mmm, I guess. But I like Holly." Morley says.

The name Daisy picks is Noelle. That's her teacher's name. So the new baby is going to be called Lily Holly Noelle Star. Morley says there'll be a Christening in a few weeks. That's a ceremony to name a baby. It happens at their church. I'm invited, if I want to come.

And the Stars also invite me to the repeat sleep-over party, because the storm meant everybody had to go home early. Except me. That's because my mother was supposed to pick me up. But she wasn't answering her phone. As usual. So I'm still here.

Right then, I know, is my chance to say I might not be in Seabright then. I start to say that. "I don't know..."

But then Eira calls us to help with the vegetables. I swallow the words. Out in the kitchen, we talk about other things.

Happy things.

Not what I'm worried might happen when my mother finally turns up.

~ ~ ~

We've boiled potatoes and then mashed them with butter. And the same, with sweet potatoes. We've cut up and boiled carrots, too. They get a brown sugar coating.

We've opened the cans of cranberry jelly, sliding the wiggly jelly cylinders onto Christmas plates. I love the colour and think, if I can have a second favourite colour, cranberry red is it. Red, like the berries and green, like my scarf. Happy Christmas colours.

We've made instant gravy out of some powder and hot water, because Eira says she doesn't have a clue how to make real gravy. Her sisters Eefa and Sorcha always do it, she says. Doesn't matter, Gus says. It's the turkey that's the main event.

He, Eira and Dom bring the turkey in from Gus' outside roaster. They unwrap the foil and inside the turkey is a buttery dark brown. It smells delicious.

The turkey goes onto a great platter and Dom carries it to the dining room table. And, with all the food arranged between us, we take our places. Dom and Gus are at the two ends. I'm sitting next to Morley and Eira is sitting across from me and next to Daisy, so she can help her cut her turkey. Daisy isn't very good at using a dinner knife yet.

Christmas dinner starts with grace, which is a sort of prayer Eira says about being grateful for food and family and friends and sharing a happy Christmas together.

one

"Even if it is by candlelight," Dom jokes, starting to carve the turkey.

"So much more romantic," Eira says.

"A real old-fashioned Christmas," Gus says.

"Like you had when you were a kid?" Daisy wants to know.

"Heavens, no. Like when my grandparents were kids. Except they were Jewish."

"YOU have grandparents?" Daisy asks, looking around as if she expects two ancient people to shamble in and join us at the table. "But where are they?"

We all laugh.

"Everyone has grandparents, silly!" Morley says. "Otherwise we wouldn't be here!"

Daisy looks annoyed, as if we're just teasing her.

We pull the crackers and everyone except Daisy puts on their tissue paper crown. She still has her princess tiara on. She puts her crown on Feather, which he doesn't like.

"Oh, poor Feather!" Morley says, pulling it off and giving him a cuddle. "Hats aren't for cats!"

"Why did the hockey player on the Turkey team get sent to the penalty box?" Gus asks, reading the slip of paper that just came out of his cracker.

"For fowl play!" Daisy shouts gleefully before anyone else can answer.

"No fair, Daisy! You can't tell the answer if you helped

make it up. You're supposed to try to guess!"

"Oh," she says. "Let me do mine next. What's the difference between a pirate and someone who loves cranberry sauce?"

"No idea," Dom says, ladling lumpy gravy onto his mashed potato.

"Give up?" Daisy asks, grinning.

Dom says sure, what's the answer?

"A pirate buries treasure and someone who just loves cranberry sauce treasures berries!"

I groan. That is just about the dumbest joke I've ever heard. Eira laughs and so does Gus. Morley just smiles. Daisy thinks it's hilarious.

Morley reads hers next. "How do you make Christmas pizza?"

"You have pizza for Christmas?" I ask, and they all laugh. I guess you can have anything you want for Christmas. Even pizza. I wonder what turkey and cranberry sauce pizza would taste like.

"Oh, I know this one," Eira says. "Christmas pizza has to be deep pan, crisp and even."

Daisy doesn't get it. Everyone else laughs. Then we explain the joke to her.

Daisy laughs so hard she just about falls off her chair and knocks over her glass of milk. Eira leaps up and rushes off to the kitchen to get a cloth to wipe it up.

"Never mind," Morley says to her. "You can have my cranberry juice," giving it to her sister and helping

Eira mop up the mess. Some of the milk has dripped onto the floor, where Feather is trying to lick it up.

Dom carves more of the turkey and the end of the knife hits something hard.

The outside of the bird is cooked. But the inside is still cold.

"Oh no!" Eira says. "How did that happen!"

"You did remember to haul out the giblets, didn't you?" Gus asks.

"Giblets?"

"Little bag with some extra turkey bits in it. Liver, kidneys, heart, that sort of thing. Folks cook them up for soups and stews. Or just to give to their pets as a treat," Gus says. "Then they put the stuffing in the inside of the bird."

"Giblets?" Eira says again. "But they're still there? IN the turkey?"

Dom starts to laugh. We all do. Then we see the stricken look on Eira's face. She really is upset.

"Sweetheart, it's all right. There's plenty of turkey cooked on the outside for now. And we can just, uh, cook the rest. Fry it or something. Later."

Eira looks doubtful.

"And I bet we'll always remember the Christmas we had to fry the bird," Dom adds, grinning.

"After we had to cook it by burying it in the backyard," Morley adds, because that's what happened. It cooked in a roaster in hot coals, buried out back.

And then everyone is laughing. Even Eira.

Morley and I help her clear the plates and get the dessert. It's Christmas pudding, which I knew about from the carols, but I always wondered what it is. I thought it might be something like the chocolate pudding cups you can take to school in your lunch. Only Christmas flavoured, whatever that is.

It's nothing like that. Turns out it's cake full of nuts and fruit like raisins, with rum sauce on top. Rum sauce tastes like rum and raisin ice cream. It's really good.

Then Dom and Gus clear the table, do the dishes and put the food away.

There's more music playing. That's me and Eira on piano, Gus on harmonica and Dom, who has some plastics from the kitchen and two wooden spoons that he's using for a drum set.

After that, there are more games, with everyone playing except Daisy. She's happy colouring.

Finally, with the Christmas tree lights flickering and going out, Eira says that's probably it, time for bed. Gus says the generator is done, at least for tonight, and he reaches to unplug it.

Dom says it's a beautiful night, how about a walk? I'd love to say yes, let's go out to see the stars. I want to keep this day going. I want it to go on and on and have my very first real Christmas never end.

I want to stand under those icy stars and make another wish.

one

I want to eat some more cookies and have another mug of hot chocolate.

I want to pull out my music notebook and write down this tune in my head, before I forget it.

But I'm so tired, I can barely make myself go brush my teeth. I don't even remember getting into my sleeping bag. I don't remember falling asleep or having any dreams at all.

After the best Christmas of my entire life.

two

Here's what people do the day after Christmas: absolutely nothing.

"It's Boxing Day," Morley explains. "That means you just do exactly what you feel like. When you get hungry, you make yourself a turkey sandwich. Or get a plate of Christmas cookies and candy and nuts and chocolate. Or a dish of peppermint ice cream."

"But why do you call it Boxing Day?"

"No idea. It's lazing around day. Today, I'm not going to make one single bracelet or work on one single pet portrait. We don't even have to start on our thank-you notes until tomorrow!"

So that's what we do. We read. Go for walks in the snow. Play with Feather and Pixel. Play music and listen to it. Dance. Laugh.

I only turn my phone on once, because I know it must

two

be getting low and need a charge. There's a message from Umma. My Mother.

There soon.

That's all.

She can take all the time she wants getting here. Better yet, never get here at all. But I don't think that's something wishing on stars can deliver.

Also, it probably isn't very Christmas-spirity of me to wish that.

"You're sad about something, aren't you?" Eira says when it's just her and me, sitting on the porch swing, watching Daisy trying to ride her bike in the snow in the backyard. Which isn't working, but no one can tell her that. And, as Dom says, it's keeping her busy trying.

"Is it that you didn't hear from your Dad? Or are you missing your mum, Sam?"

She moves closer and puts an arm around me. "You know, it's safe to tell me."

And, suddenly, I can't hold this terrible secret inside any longer. I HAVE to tell someone. Morley's Aunt Eira is like the older sister I always wanted to have. I start to talk and then it just seems like I can't stop.

I tell her about Tia Margaret, who looked after me my whole life leaving and not coming back because my mother fired her. For no reason, except that other people are going to live in our house. We're going to New York and then to Hawaii. And we might not be coming back.

Probably not, because my mother sold our house.

She listens, handing me tissues she's dug out of her coat pocket. She never interrupts.

Finally, feeling all cried-out, I just huddle against her side. Wanting to hide.

No one else has come outside. Daisy, with her princess tiara stuck on top of her pink bobble hat, is still pushing her bike around. She hasn't even noticed.

Dom and Gus are out in the garage, doing some project. I think Morley must be out there, too.

"So, let me see if I understand what you're telling me. Your mother really wants to live in Hawaii. Even though her job is mostly in the city. You might be going to music school near there?"

I nod. "But I don't think she has that job anymore," I say and explain about trying to call her at her office.

"And what does your father say about all this? Will he be in Hawaii, too?"

"No. Probably not. He lives in California with his new family. They live there because he makes movies."

"Like he's an actor? Or a make-up artist? Or a camera-operator?"

"It's not like that," I say. And then I tell her his name. And wait for the look of shock and surprise on her face.

But that isn't what I see. I can tell that she recognizes his name.

"Oh, my poor darling," she says, folding me into her

two

arms. "But I'm sure your mother knows what she's doing. She probably already has her new job there. And a plan for you both to get settled and be happy in your new home.

"It's hard, making a change to a new place, wondering if you'll make some new friends, but I know you will. And your old friends here, Morley and Jayden and me and all our family, we'll still be your friends. We'll still want you to come and visit, whenever your mother says it's OK. We won't forget you, just because you aren't here.

"And you know, Sam, things like this that look hard have a way of working out. Once you're there, it will seem exciting. Like it was when you and your mother went to Paris last summer.

"Thank you for telling me. And have you told Morley yet? Or Jayden?"

"I can't. I just can't," I sit up and start to gather the soggy tissues and stuff them in my pocket.

"I know it's hard. But I think you need to, Sam. They'll be so hurt if you don't."

I can't tell my two best friends I'm moving away. And I don't think things will just work out. Everything in me is screaming that this going to somewhere else forever is wrong. SO wrong.

Kids don't get to say that, do they? They have to just do whatever it is their parents decide for them. Just go along and try to be happy. And, if they can't do that, at least pretend to be happy. Just in case the pretending turns into the real thing.

That's what Tia Margaret says. She says you might have to fake it until you make it work.

But I think she's mistaken about that.

Fake is just fake.

~ ~ ~

I'm helping Morley do the dishes after dinner when suddenly, the kitchen light flicks back on and so does the radio. They're doing a news report that says that crews from Nova Scotia, New Brunswick, Maine, Connecticut and New York have been working around the clock. There are now only about 5,000 families still waiting for the power to come back on, the news announcer says.

"Hooray!" we shout. "The power's back on!"

And we all run around the house, turning things on or off. One of the first things everyone wants to do is charge up their phones. And laptops. And do the laundry. And have a hot shower.

Daisy has been drawing a graphic novel about a princess mermaid named Daisy who swallows a magic pink pearl. But now it's forgotten. She HAS to watch a movie on TV RIGHT NOW!

Laughing, Dom sets it up for her.

It's the next afternoon when we hear a knock on the door. I answer it and let Danny in. He looks surprised to see me here. "Sush!" he says. "I want to surprise her!"

He follows me to the living room, where Daisy is colouring. "Hey Daisy," I say. "Look who's here!"

"I'm working!" Daisy says. "I'm too busy!"

"Even for your old dad?" Danny says.

Daisy erupts from the floor, shrieking "Daddy's here! Daddy's here! Daddy's here!"

Morley has come into the room behind him. Everyone is looking at Daisy and Danny, but I see the look on Morley's face. I reach out and take her hand and squeeze it. Her dad's like mine. Not here at Christmas.

But at least I know where my dad is. In Los Angeles, at home probably with his new family, having Christmas. Morley has never even met her dad. Doesn't know his name, or where he lives, or anything about him. But I know she's been looking for him and that she never gives up hope that someday, she'll find him.

And when she does, she's sure he'll have a perfectly good reason for why he never visits or sends a gift, or a card, or even an email. Not for birthdays. Not for Christmas. Not ever.

He never even acts like she exists.

Danny has been to the hospital first to see Eefa and their new baby sister, Lily, he tells us as Daisy rips open even more gifts from him. As soon as the hospital hears that the house is warm and we're ready for them, he says, Eefa and Lily Holly Noelle will come home.

Which looks like it's now, so he calls to let them know.

Dom goes looking for the new baby car-seat and goes out to attach it to Eefa's car. He comes in muttering a while later and Eira has to go out and help him figure it out. I guess it's trickier than it looks.

Danny makes the dinner that night and stays over in one of the bed-and-breakfast guest rooms upstairs. Then he says he's taking Daisy to the city for a few days. Maybe buy her some things at the sales.

Daisy is overjoyed.

Eira and Dom are staying on here to help Eefa, that's Morley's and Daisy's mother, get settled in with the new baby. But after that, they're going on their skiing holiday. And they've got their wedding to get ready for. It's going to be this spring, here in Seabright. Daisy is all excited about being a princess bridesmaid.

Morley doesn't seem very excited about their wedding, or much of anything, really, but won't say why.

Gus is heading for the airport. He has a lady friend out in Arizona who has invited him to visit for a couple of weeks.

Morley says she's kind of looking forward to school starting again next week. She wants to hear what the pet shelter people decided, about her ideas for getting kids involved in helping the pets. And she has some new ideas for pet club.

Otherwise, she says, it's just going to be same-old. Grade 6. Selling the bracelets she makes at the market. Doing her pet portraits. Helping at home with the guests and her sisters.

two

I almost tell her how much I wish I could have same old. Same old sounds wonderful to me.

I should tell her. Now. But my mouth sort of sticks together and the moment passes.

Daisy is thrilled to be getting a trip to the city with her dad. She wants the snow to melt so she can ride her new bike. Even though that would mean her whole snow family melts away.

Suddenly it seems like everyone has plans. Things they want to get on to doing, in the new year. I'd like to have some plans, too. But I don't even know where I'm going to be living. How can I plan anything?

What I do know is that Tia Margaret won't be with us. My friends won't be nearby. We won't be in Seabright. I'll have a different home, different school, different teachers. Everything will be different.

The power is back on. The airports have re-opened. It is only a matter of a day, maybe two at the most, before my mother shows up.

And we head back to the airport.

And my life goes back to what Umma wants and what Umma gets. What she calls, "normal."

My first, magical Christmas is coming to an end.

three

BEST! CHRISTMAS! EVER! Jayden texts. He, his mum and Patrick went on a long winter ride on Christmas afternoon. It was fantastic. Bright blue sky, crisp air, powdery snow, hardly any wind at all and their horses so happy to be outside. Best ride he's had since last summer, he says.

He got an underwater camera for Christmas and their family is going on vacation to the Bahamas during March Break so he can use it. By then, he says, he expects he'll have his diving certificate, too. He's taking lessons at the pool at the university.

Morley hasn't said very much about her gifts. She says there wasn't anything she particularly wanted this year. Just an ordinary year, she says. An ordinary Christmas. She is pretty excited to finally have her own laptop and her own phone, though.

I'm pretty happy with my gifts. Especially since just

three

getting Christmas gifts at all was a complete surprise. Except the one from Margaret. She always gives me one, every year. Something else Umma doesn't know about.

Or didn't.

I'm wondering if my mother might agree to have Christmas next year. Or something like Christmas. It doesn't have to be called "Christmas." We could call it "Special Gifts and Turkey Feast Day," if she likes.

Or "Evergreen Tree with Coloured Lights and Singing Music and Playing Silly Games Day." Or even just "Winter Being Together and Having Fun Family Day."

But, try as I might, I just can't imagine my mother wanting to do any of that. No matter what we call it. When I try to picture her here, any time in the last few days, it's like I put her in the picture, sitting quietly perhaps, looking at the tree, smiling, but she just won't stay there. In my mind she just fades out of the room like we're all in the picture, but she's vanishing.

But then, there's a loud knocking at the door. Eira gets to it first and opens it, to find my mother standing there, looking impatient. There's a taxi out on the street, its motor still running and sending plumes of smoke into the frosty air.

It's cold out, but my mother is dressed in her suede jacket with a fur scarf thrown around her shoulders and her high heel boots, the kind that look pretty, but they're useless for walking in snow.

"Hurry up Sam!" she says, barely nodding at Eira.

"Grab your things, the taxi's waiting."

I don't move. Eira is saying all the polite things like, "Won't you come in, Ms. Park? It's cold out. I'm sure Sam won't take long to get packed. Can I get you a cup of tea to warm up?"

Umma brushes all this aside. She steps into the front hall, pulls off a glove and hands Eira some money. "For Sam being here during the storm," she says. "Thank you for putting up with her, Ms. Star."

Eira looks surprised. "No really, there's no need. We enjoyed having Sam here with us. It was our pleasure…"

Umma interrupts. "Sam, why are you still standing there? Go get your suitcase and backpack and coat. Say thank you to Ms. Star and Morley. I'm tired of waiting!"

Reluctantly, I go to gather my things.

When I come back, Umma is still standing in the hall. She turns away from Daisy, who's trying to tell her all about her princess bicycle. "Get in the car!" she says to me.

"A moment, please," Eira says, gently guiding me toward the living room. "There's something I need to say to Sam. In private."

My mother looks surprised and annoyed. I don't care.

Eira pulls me into a hug, once we're out of my mother's sight. She whispers, "Thank you, sweetheart. We loved having you. And we'll see you again. You can leave anything you want to here and collect it

three

later, like your jewellery box from Gus. Or let us know where to send it to you in your new home.

"Remember to write to me. You have my address and email and phone number. Also Dom's. Do that. I want to know how you're doing, though I know it will be good. You're a special girl and I know you have a wonderful future to look forward to! Good luck!"

She slips the money my mother gave her into my pocket. "For a treat, when you get there," she says. "Write and tell me what it is!"

~ ~ ~

"You're a very fortunate girl, Park Sam Hae," my mother says, as we're sitting at the departure gate, waiting for our flight. "So spoiled and I think you just don't appreciate it enough. Maybe you will get accepted by one of the music schools. I hope so. After the auditions."

"What do you mean?"

"Auditions. They decide if you get a scholarship at one school or at the other. If yes, you start in the new year."

"What schools? Where?" I say. "In New York?"

"One of them is. The other one's in Michigan, I think or maybe Massachusetts. One of those places."

Oh, I think. I'm not performing for one audition this week; there will be two. Brentwood Kings Academy, the one I already know about, and also somewhere else. Some place far from home. But what will I play for the second audition? What will they want to hear? I have only a few days to prepare. And just my violin. No piano.

"This is violin probably. No piano." Umma says. "Or maybe they want both. "One might accept you or not. If not, we'll be in Hawaii." And she replaces her ear buds.

I pull out my laptop and look up the second audition school. It looks OK. Like it used to be a rich person's home in the country that got turned into a school. Their website talks about all the sports they have, so that students become "well-rounded individuals." I don't much like sports. I only do them when we have to in gym class.

I guess that makes me not very well-rounded.

They also talk about all their events that give students "numerous opportunities to perform." And how so many of their graduates go on to professional music careers. They name some of their famous graduates, though I notice this doesn't include The Angelas. Angela Hewitt and Angela Cheng. They're my mother's favourite pianists who she says I have to work very hard to be just like.

Are these schools close enough that I can visit Morley or Jayden during vacation? If they invite me?

Then I look up to see if Hawaii has any music schools. I mean major ones, like the ones I already know I'd love to study at some day, ones like Paris Conservatoire or Julliard or University of Toronto.

Even though I already know you don't go to those schools just for their name and reputation. Or for where they are. You go because you want to work with a particular teacher, one who wants to help you grow and improve. And is already really good at what you need to learn next.

That might be technique. That's about how to get the best sounds from your instrument. It might be improving in expression, which is playing with more feeling and emotion. It could be improving your confidence in your playing.

Or improvising, which means playing music straight out of your head, not already written down.

Or composing.

Or conducting.

You choose who you need right now. And they choose you.

Teachers like my violin teacher, Anton, and my piano teacher, Sonya Clementi and Madame Boulanger care about my playing and me getting better as a musician. But Hawaii is too far away, way too far away, for me to continue to learn with them the way I do now.

5,400 miles away from Seabright. That's 8,700 kilometres. That's what it said when I Googled it.

That's further from home than I've ever been. Or ever want to be. All the way across the country and then far out into the ocean. Half a world away.

It's not quite half-way around the world, but it might as well be.

"I don't want to go," I tell my mother in the limo on the way to our hotel.

"Don't be stupid!" my mother says in Korean. "You want this, you don't want that, who cares? It doesn't matter. This is the next step of your music career. Everything we've worked for."

"My friends aren't there."

She shrugs. "So, no problem. Get new friends."

"It won't be like home."

"You're 12 years old. Almost. Not a child. But not an adult yet either. Now is the best time to start to get famous. So we must enter competitions. Win the big awards, get noticed in the music world. This is how you get invitations to perform. And recording contracts. How you get to work with many important conductors. How often do I have to tell you this Sam, You can't get famous in sad little town no one has ever heard of!"

I've heard of Seabright. I like it there. And it's not sad. Not to me.

It's special and comfortable and home. That's what I tell her.

"Enough Sam! Of course Hawaii is more special than Seabright or even New York City. That's the best reason to go. We'll have a fabulous adventure!"

But I don't want an adventure. I want to be warm. And safe. I want the teachers and friends I have now. I want my own piano. I want Tippy and Margaret. I want my home.

three

I want space to learn, to perform with the Youth Orchestra, to compose.

I want to be with my family. Like Morley has. Like Jayden has. Like Tia Margaret has, in Mexico. Only I want to be with them all, in Seabright.

That's what I want. I just don't know how to make it happen.

A message pings from Jayden. With a silly picture of Tippy, wearing sunglasses.

Hey we drove by your house and there was a moving truck there. What's that about?

Uh oh. I didn't tell him.

I didn't tell Morley, either. It's not because I forgot. I couldn't stand to see the looks on their faces. After all, what do you say to your best friends? Hey, my mom feels like living somewhere else so, sorry, I'm outa here?

But what else can I say but the truth?

That's what I tell Jayden. I'm so sorry. My mother wants to live somewhere else.

He answers right away. Where? Here? You bought a new house and didn't tell me???

No, not there. I'm sorry.

Not here? What does that mean?

Not Seabright.

Yeah? So, near here?

Hawaii.

HAWAII!!! Is this a stupid joke or something?

What can I say? It's my mother's idea. Not mine. I don't want to go. This isn't my fault. I want to stay. Could I live with your family?

There's nothing I can say that is going to make things better.

I wish. Don't want to go. No choice.

He doesn't reply.

The next message is from Morley.

You're LEAVING? And you didn't even TELL ME???

I thumb in: I'm so sorry. My mom says we have to. I just found out.

She replies right away: Your found out WHEN, exactly?

Right. When. I found out, or guessed most of it, a few weeks ago. I can't say that.

Today. From my mom. On way to airport. Total surprise!

I can't believe you're my best friend and you didn't even tell me. And Jayden says you didn't tell him, either. Did you tell anyone? I'm so mad at you, I don't even know what to say. And don't tell me this was a surprise. You must have guessed or something. Margaret must have known and told you.

I can't blame her, because she's right. I'd be mad, too, if she was doing the leaving and I was doing the staying.

three

I try to think of some good answer, but my brain just can't. I've got a headache, and my stomach hurts. I just want to crawl under my duvet and sleep and sleep and sleep. And maybe never have to wake up.

Because this is the worst thing that's ever happened, in my whole entire life.

four

But I do wake up.

We're in a hotel room, a suite that looks just like all the other places we've ever stayed. I go check on my mother. She looks small, a stick figure at the middle of a huge bed. She still has her sleep mask on. I close her door as quietly as possible.

Then I shower, get dressed and phone room service for coffee, yogurt and fruit for my mother and pancakes with whipped cream and strawberries on top and orange juice for me.

I sign for the breakfast, adding a tip to the bill. I eat, then find some note paper in the desk drawer and write my thank you notes.

Every gift comes with a cost, Tia Margaret says. Even if the cost is as small and simple as having to create a gracious, written thank you.

four

The first one is to Morley's Aunt Eira. I thank her for everything she and her family did to make it a happy Christmas for all of us. I tell her how much it meant to me to be there, with them all; how fun it was, even if there was no electricity. I say I hope she keeps up playing the piano, because it looked like she was enjoying it.

The second one is to Uncle Gus. I thank him for the beautiful jewellery box he made for me and for showing me the stride piano playing. I say I'd love to learn some more about playing jazz piano and that maybe some time I'll get that chance.

The third one is to my violin teacher, Anton. I thank him for working with me for so many years, but my mother is taking me on a vacation. I don't know how long I'll be gone. But I'll let him know when I find out. And maybe there is another student who needs my lesson time slot on Thursday evenings. I apologize for how sudden this is. I thank him again for lending me his ukulele.

The fourth letter is like the third one, except to my piano teacher, Sonya Clementi. I tell her a little about the auditions and promise to let her know what happens.

My final letter is to Mr. Cadeau, thanking him for letting me into his French class, and also for the Learning Plan he helped put together for me. But I don't think I'll be back to your class next week, I say. My mother wants us to travel and I'm not sure I'll come home to Seabright or to Evangeline School.

I find five envelopes in the desk drawer and address

them. They'll have stamps for sale down at the front desk.

Later, I'll send them each a short email, saying pretty much what's in the letters. The emails will get there a lot quicker. But it doesn't replace a written thank you or explanation. A note you write makes the thank you or the news real and also shows consideration. Tia Margaret taught me that.

By the time I'm done with the letters, I hear my mother moving around in her room. I've eaten the breakfast and the coffee is probably cold by now. It's almost lunch time when Umma finally appears, saying she's going out with some friends and she'll be back in a few hours.

I can watch a movie or practice or whatever I want to do, she says.

I send a sorry message to Morley. And one to Jayden.

I go down to the front desk and mail all my letters, then to the gift shop in the lobby to buy post cards and chips and a chocolate bar.

Back in the room, I write the postcards. One is to Dom, because it has a giant gorilla on it on the top of the Empire State Building. I know he likes old horror movies.

One is to Patrick, and it has some horses. Just to say again how much I loved the horse-riding lessons last summer.

There's one for Morley and another for Jayden, saying, "Sorry."

four

The last one is to Uncle Gus, thanking him again for showing me the stride piano playing. Now I know it's a type of early jazz. I'm planning to get some jazz piano lessons, wherever we end up next.

Then I have another look at my phone. And my email inbox.

Nothing new there.

I send a Miss-You message to Margaret.

She answers right away.

Miss you too, mi corazón. Must start new job Mrs. Tomlins-Cooper next week. She has three little boys. Good luck with lesson Madame.

I write and tell her about the auditions. But I can't say much. I don't know much about this second audition that I have to do. I wish Margaret was here so we could talk. Or not. I need her. She could help me figure out so many things.

One of them is what am I going to do about these auditions that I don't want to pass? I could play really badly and totally blow the auditions. Say I was nervous or something.

But if I do, it will dishonour my teachers. And my parents, who have paid for my music lessons, as Umma never allows me to forget.

I could play my best. And maybe get into a school that at least isn't as far from home as Hawaii. That would please my teachers. And Umma.

But can I do that? My heart just isn't in going away to school. Even if it's a really good school that helps you get into Julliard or the Conservatoire, as their websites say many of their graduates do.

I could play just sort of medium-OK. But what's the point of doing that?

I flick on the TV. It's a giant screen. They've got a lot of movies on there, but not any I want to see. Or see again, like The Wizard of Oz or Toy Story 3.

I pull some music scores up on my laptop. It helps to look at a piece and sort of think it through. Imagine playing it in your head and feeling it with your body. It's something you don't need a piano to be able to do.

Then I practice my violin for a while.

But it just isn't sounding right today, or maybe I'm just not my usual playing self today. I don't know. After an hour or so, my violin goes back into its case.

I check my phone. No messages.

Look at my laptop again. No emails.

Look outside. Just lots of traffic and people walking on slushy streets.

Pull up the score of the music I have been composing. I call it Concerto in D Major. Concerto just means a piece of music on the piano. It can be any length.

D Major is the key signature with two sharps. It's happy and bright. I just like it. And I think it fits what I want to say in my first concerto. It's about what it felt like to be in Paris last summer and also what it felt like to be at Morley's for Christmas.

four

I've got the first movement pretty much the way I want it. But there's sort of a hole in the second movement that I want to work on. And the third movement is just a couple of ideas right now that don't quite fit together.

A movement is just a chunk of the music. Like a chapter in a book. Or maybe more like one short story in a collection of short stories that are all related to each other. The whole book of stories is like the whole concerto. Words telling a story. Or sounds telling a story. Or several stories that belong together.

Taking you to a place. Giving you an experience. Letting you see, through the composer's eyes.

Philip Glass said in this article I read about him that he composes in hotel rooms. He's a famous American composer. I guess he travels so he can play his own music; he didn't really say what takes him away from home. Just that he likes to compose in hotel rooms.

If he can do it, I guess I can, too.

Except I don't have a piano. He's probably got one of those keyboards that fold, or you plug into your laptop or something. Or maybe the hotel people always put a piano in his room.

I could call down to the desk and ask if they have a piano somewhere they could send up here. Or if they have a ballroom with a piano I could use during the day to practice. My mom would probably be OK with that.

I do have my laptop, with my composing software on it. I work on it, imagining I can hear the music, playing with my fingers on the edge of the table as if it has piano keys.

I don't even notice anything around me when I'm composing. It's like I'm inside the music. In a whole music bubble where nothing else exists except a world of sounds, like great swirls of colours.

Then the door opens, breaking the spell, and my mother is saying, "Sam, what about dinner?"

"Um, dinner?" Is it that time, already?

"Well, find your coat. We'll go out. Get something. And the piano I ordered isn't here yet?"

She looks around, as if I might have hidden a piano somewhere.

"No," I say. "But it would be wonderful if I could have one."

Umma stops at the front desk to ask about a piano.

The clerk, the same friendly young guy that sold me the stamps earlier and said he'd mail all my letters and postcards, asks Umma if she wouldn't mind waiting, just a moment. So sorry for the inconvenience. He turns and disappears behind a door, coming back a moment later with an older woman with very short hair that is the colour of Margaret's favourite cooking pots.

"Ms. Park and Miss Park, if you'd just step over to the side for a quiet word?"

"Of course," my mother says.

There's a problem. My mother's charge card has been

declined for something she signed for in the gift shop. That means, her card didn't work. Whatever it was she got in the shop isn't paid for.

"Try this," Umma tells the front desk manager, handing her a different card. The woman takes it, nodding, then returns it with a stiff smile.

We walk out the front door of the hotel and I look around, wondering which way we should turn to find a restaurant. One she'd like, meaning they give you lots of little plates, each one with a tiny little bit of something and where maybe I can get what I want, which is a hamburger and chips.

But instead of saying anything about dinner, my mother grabs the arm of my coat and hauls me along, down an alley and back into a side door of the hotel. It looks like the door that staff people use.

"Quick!" she says. "Hurry up Sam. Stop dawdling!"

I follow her up the stairs and back to our room, where she tosses clothes and shoes and makeup into her suitcase and tote bags, not bothering to fold things, like usual.

But why?

"We're leaving now. Never coming back. They're very rude people here. It's shameful!"

So, I guess we aren't staying here. I do what she says. Then we have to run down the fire escape stairs and back outside in the cold, lugging all our stuff. The wheels of her suitcase skitter in the slush.

We walk, as fast as we can, for a few blocks.

She hails a taxi. This one takes us to another hotel. It's smaller. It doesn't look like a place that might have pianos they can send up to our room.

There's a dusty sign on the elevator that says, "Temporarily Out of Order."

I trudge up the stairs behind her, half carrying and half dragging both our suitcases.

Every single thing in our new hotel room is beige or brown or black. It has a funny smell. There's only one bed.

"We won't be here long," Umma says. "Then," she says with that dreamy happy look she gets a lot lately, "we'll be in Hawaii."

We dump our stuff and go searching for a grocery store. The room has a microwave and a little refrigerator. We get rice bowls and coffee creamer and a bag of oranges and instant oatmeal. Dinner for tonight, Umma says. Also food for tomorrow.

"After that, I'll call your father.

My father? But he's in California, I say.

"He'll send us some money," Umma says, settling back with the remote control. "Like always. No worries!"

Then she settles down to do something on her computer. Work, she says. She's careful not to let me get a glimpse of the screen.

But I think I know what's on it. And why we're in this crummy room.

five

"*Ah, non, Cherie*," Madame Boulanger says. "*Non*, this is not the way. Allow me to show you." I pause, allowing my bowing arm to relax and my chin to release my violin.

"Try, if you please, *comme ça*." She raises her bow and demonstrates and yes, the way she shows me is both smoother and gives a richer, deeper tone. There is a singing quality to her playing that I am always trying to achieve.

I try it.

She shows me again.

I try again.

After several tries of just these two notes, she says, "*Bon*. This is improved. We move on."

I play the Gershwin Concerto in F, the violin part.

"*Oui*," she says at last. "This is good. Now, you go to the piano."

I do, repeating it twice. She stops me many times to suggest a different fingering, or that something should be a bit louder. Or softer. Or convey more emotion.

And then, to my surprise, she joins me, not to criticize my playing but to play the violin part while I play the piano part. Playing together is always my favourite part of a master class with Madame, but it so rarely happens.

"And now, I think, the Haydn," she says.

I play the Piano Trio No. 43. It also has a violin part, but I haven't learnt it yet. She stops me a few times to make comments and corrections. I love these Haydn pieces, especially knowing he wrote them for young women like me to play. In his time, long ago, women couldn't have a music career, but many did play, very well, at home for their families and friends. Haydn understood them and wrote songs for them to enjoy performing and showing off their skills.

"And your encore piece is?"

I play the largo from Keyboard Concerto No. 5 by J. S. Bach.

"Tell me, what is it you are feeling when you play this?"

Sadness, I think. Longing. "*Ma maison*," I say. It means my home. "Missing it."

"Yes. Yes, I see this, truly. And, perhaps more?"

"The third movement. It is fast, rushing, getting

somewhere."

"And yet, you have not played this for me."

So I do. And feel, all the way through, that sense of running towards something I want, very much. But just can't quite get to.

"And the first movement, the Allegro moderato? You've learnt it also?"

"Not well enough yet, Madame, to play for you."

"I see. But perhaps I can hear it next time, yes?" She glances at her watch and I know our time together is nearly over. We have gone through all of the pieces I have been working on. She has offered corrections along with encouragement.

We've talked about the auditions, and what I might be asked to play there.

Madame has praised my progress, which makes me happy and a bit less nervous about the audition coming up.

"Do not worry yourself about the judges," she says. "They listen for talent. For potential. For promise. And you, my dear, have all of these in great abundance, especially for one so young. You need only do your best.

"In a moment, I will call maman to join us and discuss matters, *ma chère*. But first, perhaps you would play for me a piece of your choice? Is there, perhaps, something you are working on you might show me?"

"*Oui*, Madame, there is. It is this," I say.

I play the first movement of my Concerto in D Major.

She sits, listening intently. I have no idea if she likes it. Or is merely waiting for me to stop playing.

As the final chord fades, I lift my hands to my lap, awaiting her judgement.

"Bien. This is interesting. *Un soupçon* of Haydn, I think, but also the echo of Gershwin, an unusual combination, *n'est-ce pas*? Pleasing, and yet strangely I cannot place this music, Sam. What is it?"

It is Concerto No. 1 in D Major, I tell her. By Sam Park.

"Indeed," she says, smiling broadly. "And so, it seems, my dear Sam, you are a composer!

We talk a bit about how I can get lessons in composition. About my teachers at home, Anton and Sonya and what they are working on with me.

Madame asks me what I want music to be, in my life.

She asks as if she really wants to know. The true answer.

"Composing," I say. "I want to perform, yes, but mostly I want to compose music. And, maybe, teach. Some day."

"And there is also something else, no?"

"I don't want to go away to a music school. At least, not yet."

"You want to stay in your village – this Sea-bree?"

"Seabright, yes."

"And why is this your choice?"

"I like my teachers there. All of them. And my friends. And it just feels like the right place for me to be right now. As long as I can still have lessons with you, as we do now? And come to Paris again in summer? That was *splendide! Superbe! Magnifique!*"

"Ah, *oui*. But go on, Cherie."

"Because…I can feel there. I can think. And, my home. It's near the ocean."

She smiles. "*Oui. Je comprends*. It is, just now, *le village de ton coeur*?"

The village of my heart.

"Yes. It is. The place where I hear music most clearly. In my head. Where I can work."

"But at this school, they teach composition. And much else of use to you, I think. It is more about music and less of the standard school subjects."

"Perhaps for me, but not yet," I say.

"It could be that you are right. But here is my advice to you, wherever you are. Use every experience. Pour it into your music. *C'est si bon*."

Yes, I think, it is good.

"Three hours of music work each day is sufficient. And in the other time – you dance. You dream. You do all the things young girls do.

"Tell your mother this most emphatically. And I will see you again, Sam. This I promise you. Your mother knows how to contact me – but perhaps you will write to me now and then yourself. Reach me here!" She hands me a card with her New York and Paris phone numbers as well as her email address.

"I am in America at this time of year. Or in Paris, as you know, in summer. Always, you can reach me here. Or there.

"One more thing I must say to you before your mother joins us. It is this: many can play beautifully. Brilliantly, even. But you, I think, have a gift beyond this. You can choose to play very well, among the best in the world. Or you can be the best at your own gift. What is it to be, Sam?

"Think on this, until we meet next." She picks up a bell next to her water glass, shakes it, and her assistant comes into the room. "Élodie, tell Madame Park, if you please, that I request her now to join us," she says.

My mother enters and arranges herself on a nearby chair. Élodie offers tea or coffee, but my mother waves her away.

"Madame," she says anxiously. "Sam will gain acceptance at Brentwood School? Or the other? And a scholarship?"

"This is not for me to decide," Madame says switching from French to English so my mother can understand. "But let us talk of how you support your daughter in her music."

"She practices every day for five hours. Some days more," my mother says. "She must work very hard for a music career!"

five

"Five hours? Five? But this is not good, at so early a time in her life. For someone older, yes. Not yet," Madame says, alarm in her voice.

"Perhaps, each day, some practice. Some theory. Some composition. Three hours, this is the most that is wise for the *jeunes filles*. Today, piano. Tomorrow, violin. This gives young hands, young bodies time to stretch. To grow.

"The young girls, they also need time to be themselves, more than musicians. To read books. Go to concerts. Giggle with friends. Go to movies. Too much work too soon, it can damage the young talent!

"This is most important, Madame Park, to remember. The prodigies, like your daughter, they are musicians, yes. But also people, girls, becoming young women. Learning who they are, as artists. As people."

Umma is stony-faced, her lips a tight line.

And then, with the briefest of good-byes, my mother has shoved me out of Madame's suite and is propelling us both towards the elevators. I barely have a chance to thank Madame. And her daughter, my friend Élodie.

Umma is angry. "That's absolutely the last time, Park Sam Hae. That woman! She says you don't need to practice. Instead, you should giggle! So stupid! Do the Angelas do that? Read books? Go to movies? No. We pay for a master class. That woman is supposed to be teaching you how to become a World class performer. Not that other foolishness! We never want her again, Park Sam Hae. Never! There's no reason to go back. It's just a waste of money!"

I expect my mother to come up to our room with me, but when we get to our hotel, she hands me the room key card and says "You go. Eat something. Get ready for your audition. I'll be back soon," and she turns to hail another taxi.

So I eat a noodle bowl and some oranges. Practice my violin. And imaginary piano, on the side of the table. And watch some movies. And email everyone, but Margaret is the only one who answers.

I pretend to be asleep when my mother finally comes back.

six

We've been waiting, parents and kids or teenagers, for what feels like a really long time.

We've all been offered practice rooms, to warm up. They're like little closets where you can do some scales or breathing exercises or whatever it is you need to do to get ready to play.

I've already done that.

Now, Umma and I and some other kids and adults are sitting on wood chairs in a sort of hallway. We can still hear the kids who are still warming up in the practice rooms.

It's like waiting for the dentist.

The parents are saying things like "Just breathe, darling. Breathe!" and "Remember what I told you about…" and "I'm sure you'll do just fine. You always do!"

My mother isn't saying anything. She's just sitting there next to me, playing a game on her phone.

A woman appears. A name is called. Someone gets up to follow her.

The rest of us wait.

I review my music in my head. Hearing it. Hearing myself play it. Feeling the bowing, the fingering, softening my shoulders, making my wrists liquid.

Emptying my mind of everything except this music in this moment.

Reminding myself of the fingering Madame showed me. The bowing. And what she said.

Time passes.

Then my name is called. I follow the woman inside. There are three adults, two women and one man, seated in a row behind a table. On the table are a glass jug of water and three glasses, half full. There is a black grand piano. A music stand. And nothing else.

"Good luck," the woman who walked me in here says. She goes to sit next to the door.

"Good afternoon, Miss Park," the older woman sitting in the middle says. She has a lot of frizzy white hair and heavy black glasses. "I am Patrice Ellis May, of Brentwood-Kings Academy. These are my colleagues, Daniel Nottingham and Dorothea Ling.

"It is a pleasure to meet you. And play for you," I say.

"Madame Boulanger has kindly provided us with a list

six

of pieces you have studied," Ms. Ellis-May says. "We will choose three selections from this list. One for violin. Two for piano. Finally, you may play one selection of your own choice, on either instrument. Do you understand?"

"Yes, Ms. Ellis-May," I say, taking my seat at the piano. "Thank you."

"We are very much looking forward to hearing you play the Haydn," she says. And so I play it.

There is absolutely no reaction from my audience of three. Though I do see them writing some notes.

The man, who looks like the youngest on the panel, has a lot of floppy black hair that he has to keep brushing away to be able to write. "And now, the Chopin, please," he says.

I play it.

"And our final choice is the Brahms Piano Trio No. 1 in B Major," Ms. Ling says. "The violin part from the first movement, please."

I open my violin case, remove it and my bow, arrange my chin cloth, check that the strings are in tune, make a slight adjustment, pause and then start to play.

"Thank you, Miss Park," Ms. Ellis-May says afterwards. "And your final selection will be what?"

"My own composition," I say, naming it. "The first movement, Allegro." Because it means "joy."

I play it with the passion Madame encouraged. With abandon. With the true joy I had with Morley and her

55

family. And playing with Madame.

This kind of playing is harder. Riskier. But what do I have to lose? For once, I play without any barriers. Allowing myself to be carried away in the music, as if I am the only person in the room.

Because, by now, I know they've already made their decision.

As I have made mine.

I finish feeling like I have put everything into this performance. Everything I am, as a musician. And a composer.

There is no reaction, other than a polite "Thank you," as I shake hands with each of them in turn, thanking each by name. Doing this helps me to remember them, for the thank you notes I will write as soon as I get back to our room.

"You did well, Miss Park. You will receive our decision in a few days," Ms. Ellis-May says as I am dismissed.

All there is to do now is answer my mother's endless questions about what happened.

And wait for the result.

"We can go out for a celebration I think," my mother says, surprising me. "There's a good Korean restaurant near here! And you can tell me everything about the audition. Also everything Madame said!"

My stomach rumbles and I groan, but Umma doesn't notice. Korean food is OK, some of it. I like the barbeque beef. And bibimbap. That's a hot rice bowl with vegetables and some meat or chicken and an egg

six

on top. It's pretty good. Usually. But what I'm hungry for is a big platter of chicken wings, chips and a strawberry milkshake.

Will I get into Brentwood School? If so, will I go? Would I like it there? And what would it be like, to go to a school where everyone is a musician, where every day is all about music?

Or are we going to Hawaii, to a future I can't even imagine? Learn surfing, visit volcanoes, go to real luau parties or whatever else you do there?

Or is there some way, any way at all, that I can just go home, study and work as I do now, and have my home, my music and my friends around me?

Thinking this, suddenly I'm not so hungry anymore. I push my food around my plate, while Umma picks slowly at her food like she always does, talking about how excited she is to be going to Hawaii, where her new boyfriend, she says, has a beautiful condo right on the ocean. And I'll have my own room.

That is, if I don't go to the Brentwood-Kings Academy school instead. Or the other school I have to audition for tomorrow. Where I know it will be just like today, except three different people will be the judges.

~ ~ ~

There are some people, maybe a lot of people, who think that if you're a music prodigy, that music is just really ridiculously easy for you.

Almost as easy as breathing.

But this isn't true. You might have perfect pitch, like I do, meaning I can hear a note and know what it is. Wolfgang Amadeus Mozart had perfect pitch. He's the music prodigy from long ago that other music prodigies always get compared to. There are many others, of course, but Mozart is the one that everybody is always holding up as a model. We're all supposed to be little Mozarts.

Like me, he started playing music really young. Not the piano, because it didn't exist yet when he was a child. When he was a child, he played an instrument that also has a keyboard, called a harpsichord. The sound is different and not nearly as loud as a piano. But you can play harpsichord music on modern pianos, which is what his music is usually played on today.

Mozart also had perfect recall. That means he could hear a piece of music played once and then sit down and play it perfectly, start to finish. I can't do that. I have to work really hard to memorize a piece of music.

He was a true genius, starting to compose music when he was only six years old. I'm not a genius. Just good at music and a few other things, like learning languages.

I think part of being a prodigy is finding out what you can do, what you have to work hard at, and what you just can't ever do. Or maybe never. Explore the nature of your musical gift is how Anton puts it. He says musicians can spend their whole lives exploring

six

their gift, developing it and nurturing it.

Or, he says, ignoring it. This is also a choice. A choice that, sometimes, I might feel like making. When I'm tired. When my mother is nagging me to work harder. When I don't really like the piece of music I have to learn to play.

I could just be a regular kid, except for music. Find out what that's like.

Not be what they call me at school, the music nerd.

The weirdo Asian music nerd. Who just thinks she's so smart.

The spoilt rich kid.

"Ignore them. They're just haters," Jayden says. "What do they know?"

"I think they're just jealous," Morley says. "There's nothing special about them. They probably wish there was."

I remind myself of all this, when I'm wishing that I wasn't alone in this hotel room. Another hotel room. Possibly the ugliest one I've ever seen.

If I wasn't any good at music, I'm pretty sure I wouldn't be stuck here.

It was on one of those days in New York that my mother came back to the room, not with some food like she promised but with shopping bags of more clothes, all for her except for a yellowish-brown cashmere sweater for me that I didn't really want. It's too big for me. The arms are too long.

"You're always well-dressed in cashmere," she says. "It always means you have good taste!"

I was tired of being in this ugly room and I guess maybe she was upset about something because that's when she goes shopping and buys a lot of stuff. Anyways, for some reason we got into this big argument.

It was about going to Hawaii. Or that's how it started.

Arguing with my mother is never a good idea. That's because she never changes her mind. You can't reason with her.

"Hawaii is wonderful," she said, throwing her bags down on the floor to sort through later. "I talked to a travel agent today. She showed me places there. Beaches. You can see whales. And a real volcano! And its warm every day. No snow, ever. It's never cold! And you can swim in the ocean every day!"

I'm trying on the sweater she's handed me. The colour looks like a dish of mud with some mustard mixed in. It's awful. I fold it and put it back in the bag. Maybe she'll let me exchange it tomorrow.

I can swim in the ocean at home. And see whales in summer. But we don't have volcanos.

"And what about music there?" I say. "Who will I be studying with? And how will I get back to New York to have master classes with Madame?"

"Forget Madame!" Umma says, pulling out her e-cigarette stick, fiddling with it to make it turn on and taking a puff. "What a stupid woman!"

"She has helped me. A lot. And…"

"No, Park Sam Hae. I'm telling you, I don't want to hear that womans' name again. Ever!"

"So, who will I study with?"

She shrugs, waving her vaping stick around as if she's drawing pictures in the air. "We get there. Find out who teaches. My Phillip will help. Very easy!"

As if it hardly matters. This is odd, because she has always pushed so hard for me to have excellent teachers. To be the best, the youngest, the one who will win music prizes and an international career, before I'm 20. Which is in only a little more than eight years. As she is always saying, no time to waste!

"Well then, in that case, what I want to study is composition. And jazz."

"What!" she says. "You're classically trained. You play Mozart. Bach. Beethoven. That's all that matters."

"No," I say, bracing myself for the explosion I know is coming, "it isn't. I love these composers, but they aren't everything there is in music. There is so much more!"

"Wrong! For you, playing the great classical masters is what you must do. Play brilliantly. This is what I've worked for. Given my whole life for. All for you. A dutiful daughter. You will obey my wishes!"

"I do play the classical masters' works. I am your daughter. Your dutiful daughter. But I also want to learn about other kinds of music. And I want to compose. I DO compose…"

"No you don't. Other kinds of music are just rubbish. And forget composing. There haven't been any women composers, ever."

Even coming from my old-school mother, this is stunning. Unbelievable.

Other music means nothing? Only classical music has value?

And women can't compose music? You have to be male to be able to do anything with music except play it?

That's crazy!

"Clara Schumann," I say. "A famous, brilliant composer. I love her Piano Trio!" A piece I've just started to learn.

"Only famous because she played piano. She almost always played the works of her famous husband, Robert Schumann."

Not true. Yes, she worked hard to gain the popularity of her composer husband's music, but she also composed her own music. Beautiful music. And played it, in concert. My mother doesn't want to hear this.

"Fanny Mendelsohn Hensel," I say. "Her lovely Walking Music!"

"And who ever records her? Who goes to see performances of her music? She's only famous because she was the sister of a truly famous composer Felix Mendelsohn."

"Frederick," I say. "And that's so unfair!"

six

She shrugs. "Just the truth. The real world. Get used to it!"

Yes, it's true, Frederick Mendelssohn was far more successful than his sister. Maybe because back then most people thought the way my mother does now.

"Mozart's sister, Nanerl. She must have been a tremendous pianist. He wrote his Concerto No 10 for Two Pianos in E Flat Major to play with her. I've looked at the scores and BOTH parts are really challenging!"

"Same thing. She was only the sister of true genius. Totally forgotten today."

"Barbara Pentland," I say. "Barbara Strozzi. Alexina Louie. Alma Deutscher. Louise Farrenc."

"Never heard of them," Umma says. "No one has."

"Sarah Slean. A modern musician, singer, composer and she has her own show. On the radio."

"Just proves my point," Umma says. "She has to do many different things, just to earn a living. Female composers make no money."

"Or maybe she chooses to do different things in music. Maybe they are all the ways she uses her talent. Her gift. Her skills."

Umma shrugs.

"Nadia Boulanger and Lili Boulanger." They were sisters who were both successful performers and composers. Nadia also became a famous teacher. I think they are Madame's great aunts. Or maybe cousins.

"We aren't talking about HER!" my mother says. "And forget about women composers too. Do they get invited to perform with the top orchestras? Get contracts to record music? Do they ever teach master classes at the best universities? Are they famous?"

"Yes, they do, today." I say, no longer caring how much this irritates my mother. It's simply the truth, whether she likes it or not.

"One more thing you need to think about," she says with the look that signals she's going in for the final face-slap comment. "Maybe they're women, but they're all white. Not like you. Not like me. White people. Some might be Chinese. Japanese. But none are Korean, are they?" She turns back to her phone as if we're done talking. I'm not.

"Young-ja Lee," I say, triumphantly. "South Korea's most famous composer!"

"No one ever heard any music by him."

"Her!" I say, triumphantly. In English. And, right in that moment, I know I'm never, ever, going to speak to my mother in Korean again.

English is the language of MY home. My country. My culture. My life.

ME.

English and music, these are the languages that I think in. Dream in. Compose in. Even though I love the musical sounds of Spanish and of French.

These are my five languages.

English. Music. Spanish. French. Korean. In that order.

six

Of them all, Korean comes last, because I can use it with only one person. Or have, until now.

But no more.

Umma doesn't seem to notice that she's still speaking Korean to me. But I'm answering her in English.

"Girls or women can compose, just like they can conduct an orchestra. Not just sit there, playing something. Reading the music. Waiting for direction."

"Ridiculous! It is a stupid idea to have girls conducting orchestras. It will never happen!"

"Marin Alsop," I say, naming the first woman musician to conduct a major American symphony orchestra. That happened in 2007 when she was named the new conductor of the Baltimore Symphony Orchestra.

"There are so many great women conductors. Sian Edwards. Jane Glover. Xian Zhang. Han-Na Chang. Alondra de la Parra. Barbara Hannigan. Nadia Boulanger. And there are more…"

"So what? Who cares? People only want to hear works by famous composers. Mozart. Chopin. Brahms. Bach. Beethoven. All men. Only men. Audiences want to see fine orchestras with conductors who are men. Leonard Bernstein. Aaron Copeland. Henry Mancini. Itzhak Perlman. That's what people pay money for."

"And not The Angelas?" I say, deliberately challenging her as I never have before. Because I can no longer pretend it doesn't matter, what I think. What I need. What I want.

The Angelas, Angela Cheng and Angela Hewitt are

fantastic. I love how they play. But I'm not them.

"The Angelas are great performers, very great. The reason is they are specialists in music by men. The great men, Chopin, Bach, Mozart."

"That isn't what I want. Or not only that."

"You're still a child. How can you know what you want? I tell you what you want."

"You said I'm not a child anymore. I'm almost 12...."

"So why are you still acting like a spoilt child, rather than the dutiful daughter you must be?"

No, I think, that's not true. There is no answer to this. I turn away. It is impossible to reason with her.

"So now, you tell me, everything Madame Boulanger said. Every word."

"I thought you just said we're never to say her name again."

"Never after now. Tell me!"

"Well, I walked in, she asked me what I've been learning and what I want to play first..."

My mother pulls back a hand and slaps me. Hard.

She's never done that before.

We both stand there, shocked.

I sit down. Put a hand to my cheek, feeling it starting to throb.

I tell her I played this. I played that. Madame corrected this. And that. Just the things that were said. Just what happened. On the surface.

Just the facts. But not what they meant. To me.

All the time, singing in my head, while I talk to my mother, while we go out to get something to eat, later reading in bed and falling asleep and into my dreams, I can hear Madame telling me, in French, "Sam, *tu es un compositeur*!" You are a composer.

"AND a gifted musician. A beautiful pianist. And violinist. And so much more!"

In my head, I hear Madame saying these words.

"Remember, Sam. Remember and take heart. We meet again. Soon!"

I hug her words to me. They warm me, on this cold January night in this cold, dark city.

seven

Mom and I are in the airport again, the same one where we arrived only a week or so ago. Only this time, we're not rushing through to the exit. We're just sitting here. That's because our flight got delayed. Then cancelled. Something about a problem with one of the wheels.

Our tickets are changed to another flight. It doesn't leave for five more hours.

We're in the Frequent Flyer member lounge. I'm playing with my straw, breaking up the ice in the bottom of a glass that had orange soda pop in it.

The ice is mostly melted.

My mom has her earphones on. She's playing some kind of game on her phone. She doesn't notice when I look closer. Then watch for a while.

seven

The game asks if she wants to make bets and for how much. I watch the pop-ups in the game. They say things like "Oh, too bad! Want to try again?" and "That was so close! But don't worry, you're still winning!"

I watch for a while, pretending I'm not watching. It doesn't look to me like she's winning. Her face is set in a hard scowl.

I think she's losing this game. And the thought comes to me that it's not just points she's losing. It's real money. She's gambling.

We've been to the Frequent Flyer lounge before. This one and ones just like it at the airports for other cities. It's a sort of fancy place to hang out, when you don't like airports and those plastic chairs they have. And all the noise.

Most of the people here are men. Mostly white men. Mostly old, like my Dad or Anton or Dom.

But it's comfortable in here. And it feels safe. Or at least safer than being out in the main terminal.

In here, you can mostly ignore all my mother's getting-through-airports rules. Like walk quickly, eyes straight ahead. Don't stop. Don't dawdle. Don't talk.

And, especially, don't look like you have anything worth stealing. Which is why her good jewellery is in her purse. It's one of her designer ones, so it's at the bottom of what looks like an ordinary department store tote bag. The kind made to look like leather, but they're really plastic.

In airports, or on the street in cities, you have to be

vigilant, my mother says.

This means being aware. Street-smart, she calls it.

Never look like you have anything someone would want to steal.

Don't say, "hello," or "please" or "thank you." Ever.

Don't smile at anyone.

Don't allow anyone near you.

Stay on the look-out for pickpockets. They're thieves who work in teams, usually. While one tries to distract you, maybe by being friendly, the other one takes your wallet. Or your passport. Or anything else they think should be theirs.

It's just the way the world is, my mother says. And the sooner I get used to it, the better.

But right now, we don't have to follow all these rules. We're in the lounge, getting free snacks and drinks, where they have big soft chairs instead of those hard plastic ones out in the terminal.

You can watch TV, though it always seems to be turned to the news channel.

Or read the free newspapers and magazines.

Or even take a nap, if you want to. It's so much quieter than out in the rest of the terminal.

A chill-out zone, my mother calls it. She says anyone who has to travel deserves this bit of luxury along the way.

Meaning her. Of course. They don't have much in

seven

these lounges for kids. And you just about never see a kid in there.

What you do see is someone dressed up like a server in a fancy restaurant, taking drink orders and delivering little baskets of chips or bowls of mixed nuts or tiny little one-bite-sized cookies. Or sometimes, there are sandwiches and yogurt cups.

We've spent a couple of hours in here, just waiting.

For a while, my mother was all excited, talking on and on like she gets.

About her new boyfriend, Phillip. He's meeting us at the airport.

In Honolulu.

In HAWAII.

He's tall and handsome. He's rich, because he made a lot of money in real estate and helping people with their investments. He's crazy about her and they're going to get married…. she goes on and on.

About how this is so important because it's been her biggest dream for so long and now it's finally coming true that we can go there and she just can't believe it and we're so lucky and blah blah blah.

"Sam," she says. "SAM! You listening to me? You might get into Brentwood-Kings School, or that other school and then it's all arranged. You'll go to the Tanner family for vacation time. Or come to Hawaii."

"What? No. No way!" I don't know any Tanner family. Are these just some strangers she wants to foist me off on?

A man looks over, scowling.

Bad kid, he's probably thinking. "Or, you don't get an offer from one of these schools and we will live with Phillip."

Live with Phillip? The boyfriend?

"Why aren't you excited! You should be so happy. So many people want to live in Hawaii. It's so beautiful there! We'll have a happy new life with Phillip. Your old friends will be so jealous!"

As if. I've quit listening.

Finally, she runs down, like she always does eventually and pulls out her laptop. She says she has some work reading to do, but it looks to me like she's just surfing. Then playing a game on her phone and sending some texts.

Who to, I wonder?

My father? The new people in our house? The new Hawaii boyfriend?

I play with my ice-water until it's just water.

I wish there was a piano here. But there isn't.

And I can't play my violin. I think they have a quiet rule in here.

So I pull out my music notebook and glance at the ideas I've sketched out, but this place feels so wrong for composing, I tuck it away again in one of the secret pockets of my backpack.

I check my phone again for messages and notice the date. Wasn't this the day Morley and Jayden and I

seven

said we were going to tell each other about our Christmas wishes, and if they came true?

That gets me thinking about what their Christmas wishes were? Morley's was probably that she could find her father and get to know him. She's wished that for a long time. But what if that's a dangerous wish? What if she can't ever find him?

Or she does find him, but he doesn't want to be found? What if he doesn't want to know her? Wouldn't that be worse than never finding him?

What if he has another family and just doesn't want her around, like my Dad does about me?

Maybe that's a wish that's better if you never get it?

And Jayden, what would he wish for? Doesn't he already have it all? A big family. A farm. His horse, Spirit and all the other horses and ponies. His new pet-sitting business. His favourite brother has come home.

I got my wish, for a chance to find out what a real Christmas is like. Even if I was just sort of borrowing someone else's Christmas.

I thumb in messages to Jayden and Morley. Just to say I was thinking about them, and wondered if their secret Christmas wish came true? And telling them that mine did, and what it was.

This makes me think that Christmas is something people have to get together to make. It doesn't just magically happen. That's the Santa story we tell little kids. Santa magically brings lovely gifts in pretty wrapping paper. With ribbons.

But Morley and Jayden and me, we aren't little kids anymore. We've learned that Christmas is everything you choose to put there, in your Christmas. Everything you plan for. Work for.

Maybe that's also true about what's in your life.

I pull out my phone and tap in a message to Margaret:

Tia, in NYC. Plane 2 Hawaii soon.

I wait, but I guess she hasn't got her phone with her right now.

Umma says if I don't get into Brentwood-Kings or that other school, we might stay in Hawaii. She wants to.

Nothing.

Hope you're with your kids and your family, Tia. Hope they're happy. Hope you're happy. Hope it's a sunny day today, in Mexico.

Tlk soon.

Another hour goes by and my mother, reluctantly, puts her stuff away and says we should go.

We walk for a ways, eyes ahead, my mother motoring along and me almost running to keep up, wondering how she does it in stiletto heel boots and really tight leather pants. I'm grateful I don't have to wear them.

We get to the security line up and I'm panting, needing a drink and the washroom at the same time. But the line snakes back and forth. Every once in a while everyone shuffles a few steps forward.

Then stops. And waits.

seven

It seems like hours to get to the front of the line.

But then, finally, we're through the security scanner. And this time there's no trouble about my violin setting off any alarms.

We join the throngs of people who all seem to be headed down the hall, around a corner, down yet another hall to the very end, gate 22F. Most of the chairs are already occupied. It's surprising there's this many people who want to go to Hawaii.

Some of them have crazy coloured shirts on and shorts and flip flops. In January. In New York. I guess they think they'll never have to go outside again until they're some place that's hot.

I wonder what they do if it's cold on the plane? Since it's going to take us until tomorrow afternoon to get there.

I don't like hot weather. It always makes me feel sort of headachey and sickish.

Umma says that's ridiculous. "Everyone likes hot weather. It's healthy."

Our flight is supposed to leave in half an hour.

There's an announcement that they'll begin pre-boarding soon.

The departure area for our flight is crowded. Umma finds a seat and says I can just stand there, next to her. "Not long to wait," she says. "We'll be boarding soon." She pulls out her phone and taps out another text.

Then, she's talking on the phone. I'm sitting close

enough to her to hear the conversation. It's in Korean.

"How is your day going, Ms. Park?" a pleasant-sounding woman asks.

"Not so good," my mother answers. "This is not a day for getting good luck."

"Oh, so sorry to hear this! Well, to cheer you up, there is now $1,000 in your account for you to enjoy. Have fun!"

"Wonderful, so good!" my mother says, instantly brightening up. "Thank you!" She ends the call.

Before she can open up her game again, I interrupt. "I, um. I need the washroom," I say to my mother, grabbing my backpack and leaving her guarding my violin.

"Oh, really, Park Sam Hae," she says, clearly annoyed even though she's already had some wine AND her chill-out pill. "Why didn't you take care of that before? Sam, you do these things just to annoy me! So go! And hurry up!"

The loudspeaker burps on and a man's voice says, "This is your boarding call for Business Class and our Elite Passenger Program, you are invited to board now…"

That will include Umma. She always flies Business Class. That's those big leather seats up front where they get fancy food and lots of glasses of wine.

I've never flown there. We never sit together, on planes. "You don't need a larger seat and no wine for children, so no use getting you an expensive seat,"

seven

Umma says. "Total waste of money!"

What I usually get is a seat further back in the plane. If I'm lucky, it's a window seat near the middle. Even with all the padding around it, I always worry about my violin getting wrecked. I tuck it under the seat ahead of me, along with my backpack. With no one to talk to, all I've got to do on a flight is look at my phone, in airplane mode of course. Or study a music score on my laptop. Or watch a movie.

Or listen to music on my phone.

Which is what I'll probably be doing, for hours and hours as we fly west, right after I go use the toilet.

I'm sitting in the cubicle, doing what you do there, when I hear two women talking. One of them is loud and kind of shrieky. The other has a lower voice. Almost like a man's. And the strange thing is, they're speaking French.

But it's not the French I know. The words are all sort of flat and it's as if they've got colds, or something. And there's a bunch of words I don't know. They have the same accent in French as Mr. Cadeau.

One of them sounds younger than the other. The older one has that gravelly sound of someone who smokes cigarettes. A lot.

The younger one is whiny.

"I'm sure I saw that Asian kid come in here," smoker-voice says. "Her with the fancy leather backpack. Might be designer. Knock-off, maybe."

"It's the real thing! Me, I have not one single doubt,"

the younger woman says. She sounds excited.

So, they've followed me into the washroom.

"*Merde*, you crazy bitch," smoking-voice woman says. "As if. Who'd give a kid a bag like that? Gotta be fake. Come on, go pee or whatever you've gotta do and we get the hell out of here!"

There's the sound of something spraying. Then the smell of something like a cleaning product. Or maybe it's hairspray.

Then splashing in the sink. "But a rich kid probably has plastic, or something..."

The hand dryer, which sounds like a plane taking off, means I don't hear the rest of what they say.

Then there are sounds of other people. But I can't hear those two.

Have they gone? Is it safe to come out?

What if they're waiting, outside?

But why would they be? They've likely already decided I won't have anything worth stealing.

And there's no way they know I understood what they're talking about.

I can't stay in here forever.

As I'm coming out of the ladies', there's a voice over the loudspeaker. Female this time and young, with a strange accent.

"Paging passengers Coquette Taylor-Abeya, Muhammed Farook Muhammed, Luc Bonneheure and

seven

Park Sam Hae. This is your final boarding call for Flight 207 to Honolulu via Los Angeles leaving from Gate 22F. Repeat, this is your FINAL boarding call. Please report to your gate for immediate boarding and departure!"

Two people rush past. A businessman and a teenage girl.

Then I notice that just about all the plastic seats that were full before have emptied.

No doubt, by now my mother and two hundred or so other people are on the plane.

The airline person at the desk, where you're supposed to show your boarding pass and then walk through, seems to be shutting down her computer.

The two people I saw running past have hurried by that desk and vanished, down the bendy hallway that attaches at one end to the terminal and at the other to the door into the plane.

I feel frozen, colder than I've ever felt. It's like my body is a block of ice and I can't move any part of it. Like I'm that Christmas turkey, frozen stiff. I can't move. I just have to wait until the ice melts.

And the plane is about to leave.

And I'm not on it.

eight

I watch as the little tractor pushes the plane away from the terminal. They're leaving without me. But I feel nothing.

Nothing at all.

My body is frozen solid.

So is my brain.

I can't just stand here, watching the plane back up, get disconnected from the tractor, turn.

Leave.

I can't do anything else.

I know my mother won't be looking out the window. Won't see me, still here in the terminal, as if my feet have become tree roots.

By now, she'll have taken another of her little pills, the ones that help with air sickness, she says. But I know what they're really for.

eight

She'll play on her phone until they ask people to switch to airplane mode.

She'll drink a glass of wine and ask for another.

She'll pull on her eye mask and settle down to ignore the take-off.

She'll fall asleep.

It will be hours before she even notices I'm not on that plane. Maybe not until tomorrow, wherever she is by then.

It occurs to me that I have to do something. I'm trying to remember what it is.

Breathe. That's it.

Breathe in slowly, saying to myself, "I am here."

Breathe out slowly, saying to myself, "I am calm."

It's something Anton taught me to do before a performance. He says it helps get oxygen to your brain.

I am here.

I am calm.

I am here.

I am calm.

I say this to myself, over and over. Finally, it feels like I could take a step. I do.

Towards the chairs. I slump into a seat.

I'm here. Alone.

I am calm.

No I'm not.

The plane has left.

Margaret is gone, back to Mexico. She's not coming back, at least not back to Seabright and our home. That home is gone. It's sold to strangers who are going to move in soon. Maybe they already have.

My friends, my school, my favourite teachers like Mr. Cadeau and Anton and Sonja, they're all back in Seabright.

Everyone is there except for Madame Boulanger. She might still be in New York. I don't know. I try to remember where I put the card she gave me with her numbers, but can't.

I'm here alone.

Alone.

The thought terrifies me.

Except for when I'm practicing, I've never been alone in my life.

Never not had my mother telling me what to do. Or Tia looking after me.

Never not known where I belong.

I try to make my brain do some thinking. I could go to the airline desk and tell them I missed my plane and can I get another ticket for the next plane to Hawaii?

But I don't have the money to pay for it. I know a ticket from here to Hawaii costs a lot. Umma was

eight

saying that. I do have some money. There's the money Eira gave me, and some I saved up, hidden in my backpack. I can't get it out and count it here. But I'm sure it's not enough to buy a plane ticket to Hawaii.

Where I don't want to go.

And I can't buy a plane ticket to anywhere I do want to go, either. They'd think it was odd, a kid buying her own plane ticket. They'd probably call the airport security or the police or something.

But there must be other ways to get home. To Seabright.

Is there a train? That could work. Nobody notices a kid travelling on the train.

Or the bus.

I see kids on the bus all the time, back home.

I get out my laptop and check.

I could take a taxi from the airport into the city. But it costs $75. Plus tip. That's too much to spend, when I don't know how much the train or the bus is going to cost.

Also, you might get a nosey driver who wants to know all about you and who you are and why you're travelling. One who notices people. And gets suspicious about a kid travelling alone.

The bus, or the train, will be much better. People just about always ignore kids on public transportation.

I find out I could take the A train from JFK airport to

Howard Beach Station. It takes 10 minutes and costs $5. And they take cash. I find a $5 bill and that's what I do. From there, I could go to the train station. But the train ticket to Boston will cost $100. That's a lot more than taking the bus.

Then I get another train that costs $2.75 and takes me to the Port Authority Bus Terminal. That takes an hour. It feels very strange. The whole time, I'm telling myself to just breathe. This is just another performance. Just the same.

Even though I know it's not.

I send an email to Jayden and to Morley when I get there. Telling them what time I'll be in Boston.

They don't answer.

I can buy a bus ticket to Boston for $16.60. When I get up to the front of the line, the ticket seller man says, "What's a kid like you doing travelling alone?"

"I'm not," I say, pointing sort of behind me. "My mom sent me over to buy our tickets. I need two. One kid and one adult."

"You're under 12?" he says.

"Yes," I say. "Eleven."

Luckily for me, there's a woman with a little fussy baby sitting more or less where I pointed to. The baby is starting to cry. "Yeah, OK," the man says. I hand him my credit card.

I use it to tap the little box but it doesn't work. "Sorry, kid. Got anything else?"

eight

I pull out a $50 bill and hand it over. He gives me the change and two tickets.

"Your bus will be leaving from platform A. It's A7. Have a good trip," he says, turning to the next person.

It's still an hour and a half before the bus leaves. And then it will be four and a half hours on the bus to get to Boston. Where I hope Eira and Dom will be waiting to pick me up. That is, if they haven't already left for their ski trip.

They have to be there. They have to. I need them to help me figure out what to do.

I can't think of who else to ask.

I go sit near the woman with the baby. But not too close.

I send another email.

By now, they must have seen it.

No answer.

I phone Jayden. Leave a message.

It looks like Morley has blocked my messages.

I'm ghosted. By my best girl friend.

It hurts. I guess she's pretty angry.

I phone Eira. Leave a message.

Then I go looking for something to eat. I mooch around the little store in the bus station. It has lots of magazines and books and touristy stuff. I stand in front of the cooler, looking for something I want to eat, taking an egg salad sandwich and a chocolate milk, and am trying to decide what kind of chips I want when a woman bumps into me, hard. She stomps on my foot.

"OW," I shout. "Watch where you're…"

"Got you!" a man says, grabbing my backpack straps.

"But that woman ran into ME," I say. "It wasn't my fault!"

"Save it for the police!" the man says. "I know what I saw you do! The pair of you. Don't try playing all innocent with me! I saw what you did!"

The man won't let go of me. The other woman is saying, in a really fake-y Spanish accent "She steal! I saw her! You find things in her bag! I try stop her, but no good!"

Two police officers, a man and a woman, tell me and the woman that we must go with them for questioning.

They ask my name. Where I am going. And why. And why I stole things from the bus station store. And where I got the fancy backpack. Did I steal it, too?

I say I didn't steal anything. I was lining up to pay for my sandwich, drink and chocolate bar when the woman stepped on me and bumped me, hard.

The woman says I'm a thief and she was just trying to stop me stealing things.

I say I've never seen this woman before in my life.

The man police officer says that both of us and our bags will be searched. The woman officer takes me to

eight

a room and says I have to take off everything except my underwear. While I do, she will search my backpack.

I must hand her my clothing so she can go through it. To find stolen goods. Or drugs.

I'm so shocked, I don't know what to do. She's standing in front of the door. I can't escape.

I do what she says.

She hands back my clothes and tells me to put them on. When I come out, she is putting things back in my backpack. My other pair of jeans, two tops, the ugly sweater, my circle scarf that Morley gave me, two pairs of underwear, my laptop, phone, charger cables, and my kit bag with hairbrush, toothbrush and my kid-sized chopsticks in their case.

But there are also some things that aren't mine. A couple of books and magazines and some chocolate bars. And some other things, in envelopes and boxes. I don't know what they are. I tell her that she's putting stuff in plastic bags that isn't mine. She says be quiet. She and her colleague will take a full statement later.

Then, I go back out and the man officer says sit here and wait. The woman officer goes off with the woman. They come back soon and the two police officers say that the woman, the one who ran into me, can go. They have no reason to hold her, but I must stay. A Children's Protection Officer will be here soon to take custody of me.

The woman smirks in my direction and walks off. I'm

sure she's stolen something, but can't figure out how she hid it, if she got the same kind of search that I did.

Then they say they are taking my statement. I have to tell them, all over again, what happened. I tell them I bought my bus ticket.

"What with?" they say.

I say my credit card.

"You have to hand it over," the man says.

Reluctantly, I do.

"Keep talking," the woman officer says. "Why were you here?"

Waiting for the bus. Got hungry. Went to buy some food. Woman hit me and stepped on my foot. Man grabbed me and called police.

"OK, little thief," the woman officer says. "We've established that you are not the daughter of that woman. So, who are you? And who are your parents?"

I tell them both again that I am Sam Park. My mother has just gone away, on business. To Hawaii. I don't know where my father is. My mother has sent me to my aunt's. She will meet me in Boston. I give them Umma's phone number, knowing her new phone will be turned off. She must still be on the plane.

I say I don't know my father's number. Or email address. Even though I do.

I give them Eira's phone number. And email address.

I ask them to get in touch with Eira. My aunt.

eight

I've said this so often now, even I'm starting to believe it.

Then a really tall, skinny woman with a huge Afro turns up and says she's with the City Children's Authority and I must come with her. She signs a paper and says to follow her. I tell her I have a bus ticket and my bus is leaving soon. I'm going to my aunt's.

"I don't think so," she says. "The store owner is sick of petty thieves like you. He's pressing charges! You'll have a date tomorrow morning. In youth court. The police will inform your parents or guardians."

"But my aunt is coming to get me at Boston South Station. I messaged her. She'll be there. And I didn't take anything. I didn't do anything wrong!"

"Shut up!" the woman says roughly, grabbing my jacket and walking towards the car park. "Enough lies."

"But I can't leave. I'll miss my bus!"

"That's the first truthful thing you've said, isn't it?" the woman says. "Because you're a runaway. And a thief." Then she tells me to get into her car and buckle up. It's old and has a lot of rust. I wonder if she's a good driver. She's a stranger, and it's not safe, ever, to get in a car with a stranger. I say this.

She grabs me and shoves me in the car. She turns on the radio, some sort of awful shouty music with a lot of swearing. She says nothing else until we park in front of a big house with peeling dark green paint. There's a broken swing set and an overflowing trash container in the front yard. One of the downstairs windows is covered with cardboard.

At the door, a big woman holding a stinky baby answers the door. There's a lot of shouting and screaming going on behind her.

"Here's the one I called about, Doreen," the Children's Agency woman, who never told me her name, says.

"Yeah, right. Get yourself in here, kid," she says.

"Um, hello," I say, holding out my hand. "My name is Sam Park. And you are?"

"Kid, I don't give a damn who you are. You won't be here long enough for me to care. Get in here! You're letting in the cold!" The agency woman is already driving away. It isn't much warmer inside.

"Dinner at 6. The other kids will show you where your bed is. Lights out at 10. You'll be gone tomorrow. Don't bother trying to make friends."

"Is there a piano?" I ask, hoping so. My hands ache to play.

"No there isn't, smart-ass. And no indoor pool or home movie theatre, either. This ain't no resort. You're in trouble. So shut up, behave yourself and we'll get along just fine!" She waddles down the hall with the baby.

I look around. I don't want to touch anything. Don't even want the bottom of my shoes to touch anything here. It looks dirty and smells like cabbage. And pee. And cigarette smoke.

I go in the front room, which doesn't have very much

eight

in it except a ratty old couch, a worn-down carpet, an old-fashioned TV and some cardboard packing boxes. I pull out my phone to see what time it is.

Two hours until dinner. I guess I'll just sit here and wait. I don't know what else to do.

Then I get a text.

It's Eira.

nine

Eira: *Sam, explain. Why aren't you with your mother?*

Me: *She got on plane 2 Hawaii. I missed plane.*

Eira: *Go to the airline's desk! Tell them what happened. They'll put you on the next plane to join your mother.*

Me: *Can't.*

Eira: *I don't understand.*

Me: *Can't go 2 Hawaii. Just. Can't.*

Eira: *So you're at the airport now?*

Me: *No. At a foster home. Afraid. Need your help. Please come and get me, Eira. Please.*

Eira: *OK. OK. Tell me exactly where you are.*

Me: *In New York City somewhere.*

Eira: *Ask the people there the name of the street. The address. What part of city – like the Bronx or Brooklyn or Manhattan or whatever. Dom and I are on way to airport now. We will be there as soon as...*

I hear the woman coming down the hall and shove my phone in the top of my backpack.

"What the hell?" the woman says. "What do you think you're doing. Gimme that!" She grabs my laptop.

"Hey," I say, trying to grab it back. "I need that. It's mine!"

"I don't care what the crap you need, kid. You don't get any kind of privileges here. I'm keeping this!" She snaps my laptop shut and tucks it under her arm. "And get in the TV room with the others. No loitering out here on your own and doing God Knows What damage to my living room!"

I look around, wondering what in this room could possibly be more damaged than it already is.

"And wipe that damned smirk off your face before I smack you!" she says, turning around and leaving the room. I follow her because I have to know what she's going to do with my laptop.

She goes down the hall and turns right at the end, into what must be the kitchen. There are two ancient refrigerators, a stove, a table with three broken chairs and not much else. There's a big pot of something cooking.

She clambers up on a step stool and reaches to put my laptop on top of the upper cabinets, pushing it back so that, from down here, you wouldn't know it's there. "And that's where it stays," she says. "Now go out there with the others until I call you for grub!"

There's nothing I can do except what she says. For now. I follow the noise to what looks like it was meant to be a bedroom. Or maybe a dining room. There's an old couch in there with places where the stuffing is coming out and a lot of dark stains. It's hard to tell what colour it was, to begin with. Some kind of flower pattern, maybe.

There's also another old TV, with a daytime TV show on it, one of those ones where everybody is dressed up like they're going to a party, but all they do is hang around at home and argue with each other. And drink a lot of alcohol. And get divorced and married. They do that a lot. Or have secret babies. Or try to murder each other.

There are two boys fighting over who gets the remote. A scared-looking girl who's maybe 9 or 10 is sitting on the edge of the couch. She looks really sad. An older girl, maybe my age but I can't tell because she has a lot of make-up on, is hassling her.

"Hey," I say. "Stop that! Can't you see she's upset?"

"Oh yeah?" the older girl snarls. "Says who?"

"Says anybody who isn't a bully. Would that be you?"

The girl tries to hit me. I duck.

"Girl fight! Girl fight!" one of the boys says, then the two of them are chanting it.

"I don't want to fight with you. Just stop picking on her," I say.

"Ewww, you don' wanna fight. Who cares what you want?" the older girl says.

nine

"I do," I say. "And I bet she does, too." I point at the younger girl, who looks even more frightened than she did before.

"And who's gonna make me? You? As if!" older girl says. But then she changes her mind about trying to hit me again. "Gimme your backpack."

"No way," I say. "Go get your own."

She grabs it. I dodge. She shoves me, and I crash into the wall, recovering as fast as I can. But it's not fast enough, because somehow, she has my backpack. And is going through it. She throws my stuff all over the room. I scramble to collect it while the boys roll around the floor laughing. One of them has one of my pairs of underpants and he's trying to use it like a slingshot.

The little girl I was trying to help is just sitting there with her mouth open.

The bully girl finds my phone. Why didn't I keep it in my pocket? I don't know. I should have. But now she's got it.

"Ah ha!" she says. "Gimme this and I'll leave you and the twerp alone. If I feel like it!"

"Don't be stupid," I say, grabbing my backpack and trying to get my stuff back in it. "That's my phone. Give it back!"

She runs down the hall and up the stairs with me right behind her. She opens a door and tries to slam it behind her, but I'm close enough to get in with her.

"This is the bathroom, you stupid creep!" she says.

"Get out!"

"I will when you give me my phone!" I say, reaching for it.

But I can't quite get hold of it. She drops it in the toilet. Which, not very surprisingly, needs to be flushed. Or probably did, hours ago.

"Oh, gross!" she crows. "The Asian kid likes to play in crap!" Only the exact words she used were worse than that. Ones I don't even let myself think, they're so ugly.

And then she flushes. My phone, with all my messages and contacts is gone.

"OK," she says. "Now get out of here, creep."

She shoves me hard and I knock my head against something. I don't know what. I'm trying to get up when she kicks me. I taste blood in my mouth and try to crawl away from her. She laughs and slams the bathroom door.

I sit there a while, feeling in my jacket pocket to find a tissue to wipe my face. Feeling dizzy and like I'm going to throw up.

At least I still have my backpack. And some of what was in it.

What I don't have is what I need the most right now. A way to get a message to anyone at all that can come and help me escape.

The bully girl stays in the bathroom so long that the two boys come and bang on the door. They say they really have to pee. She says "too bad, lousers, do it

nine

on the floor." They start to pound and howl and finally the woman comes up. She hits each of them for all the racket. Takes one look at me and walks away.

From somewhere else, I hear the baby cry. And feel sorry for it.

And all of us here in this terrible place.

The dinner is watery soup with cabbage and some kind of mystery white things floating in it. And white bread that has gray spots on it. And a glass of some kind of sugar drink, the kind you mix up with powder and water. I can't eat any of it. It's disgusting.

My mouth has stopped bleeding and I'm feeling less dizzy. I rinsed my face with cold water at the kitchen sink, when the woman wasn't looking.

After dinner, I ask the little girl, the quite sad one, to show me where they sleep. The others are all in the TV room. I have no idea where the woman and baby are.

"This way," the girl says. We go up the stairs, up to the third floor, which is just a dark hallway with four doors. She opens one. "This is the girls' room," she says. It's way smaller than my bedroom at home, but it has four bunk beds crammed into it and nothing else. All the beds have a bare mattress. No sheets or pillows. Some have a dirty blanket on them.

"Where do you keep your stuff?"

"Anywhere you can hide it. But they just find it and take whatever they want," she says. "They took away everything I had. I've just got this," she reaches in her pocket and pulls out a child's change purse. "We were out shopping and I got lost."

"And a lady said you had to come here and they'd find your parents?"

"Yeah. But that was yesterday," she says. "And I'm scared."

"Yeah," I said. "Me too. My name's Sam, by the way. Sam Park. What's yours?"

"Rachelle Leitkov."

I reach out to shake her hand, but I guess she doesn't know how to do this.

"Nice to meet you, Rachelle Leitkov. So, which bed is yours?"

"Whatever one is left when Lakeesha picks the one she wants."

"That older girl? The one who was hassling you when I came in?"

"Yeah," she says with a sigh. "Her. She got here right after me."

"And what about those two boys? Who are they and when did they get here?"

"I dunno. They don't talk. I think they might be brothers, though."

"Is that everybody who's here?"

"There were some others yesterday. But they went somewhere."

"Where?"

"I don't know. This woman just came and got them."

"When?"

"Right after breakfast. So, are you here until they can find your parents to come get you? That's why I'm here. It's my fault. I wandered off. That's what the lady here says. She says my parents are going to be really angry with me. When they come."

"I don't think so," I say, leaning over to hug her. "I think they're going to be so happy to find out you're OK."

"Yeah," she says. "I guess. But I don't want to be here. I don't want to wait for them. They're taking a really long time to get here."

"Where do you live?"

"Hey, you two. Enough of that whispering in the corner. Get back to the TV room if you know what's good for you!" the mean woman says. "Little shits!"

Reluctantly, we both walk back downstairs. Me still hugging my backpack. Still wearing my winter coat, though I'm way too hot. And thirsty, now. And hungry.

I sneak a glass from the kitchen, then go off to the bathroom. Get inside and lock the door, surprised to find it still works. Use the toilet. Get a drink. Rinse my face again. Look in the mirror. There are bruises on my face. I pull up my shirt. More bruises.

I stay in the bathroom as long as I can. Until someone else is banging on the door.

Then I sit in the TV room. The TV is on with the sound

so loud it hurts my ears. Playing one of my dad's movies. One I've never bothered to watch. It's about this guy who doesn't have a name. He keeps moving around. He lives in his car. He gets to a new town and he is on some kind of secret mission. He beats up some guys, and flirts with this woman and then there's another fight and then the guy is shooting at someone. It doesn't make a lot of sense to me.

Then the guy with no name is locked in a room and he has to get out. But I've stopped paying attention. I'm thinking, how am I going to get my laptop back and get a message to Eira, or Morley, or Jayden, or SOMEONE about coming to help me?

There's nothing I can do but sit here. Wait. Watch my dad's movie. Feel hungry. And tired. And lost.

Hope that this nightmare is going to end. That I'll just wake up, in my own bed, in my own room, in my own home, with my piano waiting. And, soon, Margaret coming in to say, "Good morning," with my breakfast on a tray. Just like she does every morning.

My body hurts. My head hurts. My stomach is rumbling. I lie on the dirty mattress, with my backpack for a pillow, my jacket for a blanket. I feel dirty and achy all over and more hungry than I've ever been. I just want to wake up somewhere else.

Except that I can't get to sleep. I hear the sounds of other people coughing and snoring. Getting up and walking around, making the floorboards of this old house squeak and creak.

I lie there and wait to sleep. Wait for the house to get quiet. Wait for – what?

nine

For help.

I just lie there and wait. And listen. And try to think.

Finally, it seems like the house is quiet. It must be really late. Midnight, maybe. Or later.

I'll get up. If anyone sees me, I'll say I got lost in the dark. I'm looking for the bathroom.

I sit up and feel dizzy again. I stay still, listening. Waiting for my head to clear and the throw-up feeling to pass.

It isn't totally dark. There's light coming in the window, through the drooping blinds, from streetlights. Or maybe it's the moon.

I pull on my coat, trying not to wince from the pain in my side where Lakeesha kicked me.

I make my way across the room, to where Rachelle is curled up in a tight ball, her thumb in her mouth. I heard her crying for a long time before she fell asleep.

"Shush," I whisper to her. "Be really, really quiet. I'm going to get out of here. Go for help. Come on. Get up really quiet and we'll go."

I'm not sure she understands. "But I can't go," she says. "My parents are coming to get me. Soon. I know they are."

"Come on," I say. "We have to get out of here. This is a bad place to be. Get up. Be really, really quiet. We have to escape. Now!"

"No," she says out loud, making me scared someone might hear. "No, I can't. I'm scared," and she starts to cry again.

"Please, Rachelle. Just come with me. I'll get us out of here." I have no idea if I can get us to safety. But I have to try. Because I don't believe for a minute that Rachelle's parents are coming for her. And I know for sure no one is coming for me. They don't have any idea where we are.

I didn't have time to tell anyone.

Or maybe I did, but I blew it. Too late for worrying about that now.

"Come on. Come ON!" I say. "We have to go NOW before anyone..."

She pulls away from me.

"I can't. I can't. I'm so scared! You go. I won't tell. I promise," she says. And she rolls over towards the wall and curls into a ball.

I hate to leave her. But I have to go. Or try, at least.

I creep down the stairs. Wincing at each creak of the stairs. Stopping to listen. But the house sleeps on.

I pause at the bottom of the stairs. The door is just down the hall. Willing my feet to walk down the hall, get the door open somehow, then run as fast as I can. To freedom.

But then what? What if I go to the police and they just send me back here?

Or somewhere just as bad? Because, they'd say, I'm a thief. And a runaway.

A criminal.

nine

No. I need an adult to fight for me. To come and get me.

Not my father, in California, making movies. He won't come.

Not my mother, on a plane. Or maybe off of it now, meeting her new boyfriend, going to his place. To party, her favourite thing to do.

Not Margaret. In Mexico with her family. So far away.

Not anyone in my family. Because I don't really have a family, do I?

Not Madame. She might have gone back to Paris by now. Or still be here, but I'd be so ashamed to tell her what has happened. The trouble I'm in.

But I can't stay here, holding the sticky railing at the bottom of the stairs. I have to do something.

Get my laptop, I decide. Get out to the kitchen, climb up somehow and get it from the top shelf.

But the step stool the woman used isn't here. Or maybe I just can't see it in the darkish gloom of the kitchen. I'll have to climb on a broken chair, and then on the counter.

I do that, hoping the chair won't break and send me crashing down. And wake everyone up, including that nasty woman.

I get on the chair. It doesn't break. Then I get on the counter. Stand on my toes. Feel around for my laptop.

It's there. But I can't quite reach it.

I try to grab it but end up just pushing it further back

on the shelf.

The longer I spend here, the more chance that someone will wake up. And see me. And then – what? Lock me in a closet? Or in the basement? Or...I don't know. Something awful, too horrible to think about. Like out of those horror movies Margaret doesn't let me watch because I get nightmares.

But this place is a real living nightmare.

Just leave the laptop, a voice in my head says. You can get another one.

Not with all my contacts on it, I think. And my Concerto in D. And all the other music I'm working on.

Leave it, the voice says. *You can get all that back. Write your music again. Just get out of here, now!*

I stand on my toes. Reach as far as I can. Stretch my arms. My hands.

And, finally, I can grab the edge of my laptop. And pull it towards me.

The floor creaks and I freeze.

There it is again. Footsteps, on the stairs. Not far away.

"OK, you little shifty-eyed shit, where are you?" the woman says. "I know you're down here. If you don't want to get a beating, you better show yourself now!"

Decision time.

Stay here and pretend I'm not doing anything?

Jump off the counter and try to run past her?

nine

I have not even a second to decide. She's in the kitchen doorway now, right in front of me, blocking my escape.

With a shout I leap forward, trying to barrel into her, knock her off guard, then run as fast as possible.

But though she's big, she isn't as soft as she looks. She reaches out to grab me. I scream, wrenching away. She lunges, but too far, and she crashes into something. I keep running along the hall, to the front door, knowing she is right behind me.

But the front door is locked. I don't have time to stop and figure out how to unlock it. I turn to the living room and haul up the broken window. There is no screen, just some cardboard. I knock it out and am climbing over the edge of the window as she catches up, grabbing at me, screaming swear words.

I turn, ball my hand into a fist and hit her, just hard enough that I get over the window edge and drop to the ground, stunned. But I have to get up. I have to run.

That's what I do. I look back at the house, see she has the front door open, she's dialing her phone, she's screaming about a robber.

I'm running for my life.

When you're travelling, plans can change.

Things can get lost.

Or stolen.

You have to be smart. To protect yourself.

Keep your eyes ahead.

Keep moving forward.

Don't stop to talk. To anyone.

Umma's rules. Right now, on a cold and dark winter night, when I have no idea where I am and I'm alone, I hear those rules in my head for how to be safe.

Wondering what to do next. When things are lost. And stolen.

And you're in a strange place.

Alone.

I run until I'm out of breath. Then I walk. As fast as I can.

Once, I stop to put my right hand in some more-or-less fresh-looking snow. Because it's throbbing. Like my head.

I have my jacket. My ugly sweater. My circle scarf. They aren't nearly warm enough. I have to keep moving to keep warm. Or find a warm place to go.

But where would that be, on these streets of mostly dark houses?

I keep walking and walking. Even though I'm tired. And so hungry. And so cold. And my feet hurt.

Reminding myself that if I'd just gotten on that plane with Umma, I wouldn't be any of these things right now.

I wonder if she's missed me yet. Or even noticed that I'm not there.

nine

I try to figure out if her plane has landed yet. I remember that it takes 16 hours and 48 minutes to fly from New York City to Honolulu on a direct flight. That means one with no stops along the way.

Then I remember that there was a stop. In Los Angeles. I have no idea how long for.

I try to calculate how long ago it was since I watched the plane pull away from the New York airport terminal. It seems like days ago. Weeks ago. A century ago.

And even longer, so much longer, since Christmas. At Morley's place.

I can't work it out. How long ago everything was. When I was safe.

All I can do is keep going.

But now I notice that there aren't so many houses. I've gotten to more of a main street. Not like in the city, exactly, but there are some businesses. A computer place. A gas station. And then, best of all, a fast food coffee and donut place that's open all night.

I go inside and head for the ladies. Lock myself in. Use the toilet. Try to clean up, as best I can. Check my backpack. My laptop is there. A lot of my stuff is missing. The best news is no one found what's in the secret pockets. That includes what's left of my money.

I pull out a $20 bill, tuck it in my jeans pocket and go up to the counter. They haven't started making breakfast sandwiches yet, the woman at the counter says, but they will soon. I ask for two of them as soon as they have them, and two hot chocolates and two honey-dip donuts.

"Oh, uh, is someone joining you?" she says.

"No," I say. "I hope not."

She gives me an odd look, but takes my money and gives me the change and the donuts. I put some coins in her tips jar.

"Thanks," she says. "You from around here?"

"No. Um, just visiting," I say.

I grab the tray and find a booth. Take a sip of hot chocolate, discover it's still way too hot and wait for my laptop to power up while I eat one of the donuts. It's a relief to see I get online right away.

First thing to do is check for messages. There are several from Eira. A few from Margaret. One from Morley; she's still mad at me and says Jayden is, too.

None from my mother.

I decide I better answer the one from Eira first. I tell her what happened. The short version. I go up to the counter and ask the woman where this is. The address, I mean. She tells me.

We seem to be the only two people there.

I go back to my seat. Start a new message to Eira. Put in the address. Say I'm OK, getting some breakfast as soon as they make it. Staying warm. But does she think she can come here and pick me up? Or just tell me how to get back there? That is, if I can stay at her house for a while. Until…

Until what?

nine

I haven't got a clue.

My Dad doesn't want me. He says it's too upsetting to his wife and his new family to have me there.

My Mother? She's more interested in shopping and playing those gambling games online and her newest boyfriend than she is in me. I really doubt she'll come all the way from Hawaii to help me.

Margaret? She's with her own family in Mexico. Or at her new job. I don't even know where that is.

Madame? No. That's not a good idea.

A couple more messages come in. One is from Brentwood Kings Academy. This is what it says:

Dear Miss Park,

On behalf of the Directors, Head and Staff of Brentwood Kings Academy, we are delighted to offer you a place at our school.

We invite you to join us…

As if, I think. There is no way I can get there. No way I can pay for an expensive school like that.

I only have a little bit of money. And no home.

The next one is a congratulations message from Madame. It makes me smile, but only for a minute. Then I think how am I going to answer this?

After all she did to help me get accepted.

I don't have a clue what to tell her.

Or anyone, really. What am I supposed to say? It's 4:58 in the morning and I'm sitting in a booth in a donut shop. Still dark outside. I'm alone. Far from home.

Really far from home.

This makes me think again about my Christmas, at Morley's with all her family.

But it wasn't my Christmas really, was it?

It was their Christmas. I just happened to be there. Because there was a storm and the power was knocked out and trees were down and the airport and all the roads were closed.

So, I was there.

Total accident.

Not like being here.

Total non-accident. All totally my own dumb fault! If I'd just followed the rules, just sat near that woman the whole time until I got on the bus, none of this would have happened.

It's then I look up and the counter woman is putting my two sandwiches on the table. Wrapped up, not on plates.

"Here you go, sweetheart," she says. "I hope things..."

Right then, there're sirens. Two police cars turn into the parking lot, their lights flashing, the sirens stopping with a *CHIRP*! I grab my backpack and make a run for it.

But I'm not fast enough.

"Not so fast!" a man police officer says, catching me

nine

as I come out the door. "We need to have a little chat, Miss!"

"No!" I scream. "No! Let me go. Let me go!"

He doesn't. No matter how hard I struggle. He's just so much bigger than me.

"Come on, now. Settle down. We're going to go back inside. We're going to sit down. And talk. Just talk. OK?"

I can't fight him. I'm so tired and hurt. I just can't fight any more.

He leads me inside. Sits down, his back to the door, indicating the booth he wants me to sit in.

I slump down. Put my head in my hands. I want to cry. But can't let myself. In front of him. And the other officer. She sits down next to me.

The counter woman brings over coffees for them. And my two breakfast sandwiches, the ones left behind when I bolted.

"OK, young lady. Let's start with name." He pushes the sandwiches closer to me.

"Sam," I say, taking a bite.

"Short for Samantha?"

"Just Sam," I say.

"Got a last name, Sam?"

"Sam Park."

"OK, good. I'm Sergeant Ken Martin. This here's Officer Stephanie Lopez."

"Nice to meet you," I say, shaking their hands. Even though it isn't. Because they're going to take me back to that awful place. As soon as they look up my name on their computers and find out I got in trouble for being a thief.

"So how old are you, Sam?" Officer Lopez asks.

"Eleven," I say. There's no point in lying. They're just going to find out anyways.

"Eleven," Sergeant Martin says. "That's pretty young for you to be out, cold night like this? On your own? Want to tell us about that?"

"No." I have a feeling he isn't going to like this answer.

He doesn't.

"Your parents know you're here?"

"No."

"That's a fancy backpack you've got there. Fancy laptop, too. Not cheap."

"No."

"Didn't steal them, did you?"

"No."

"No," he says thoughtfully. "Well, Officer Lopez, what do we think? Should we leave the young lady here to finish her sandwich?"

Yes! Please, yes. Just leave me here. "I'll only stay until, um, until it gets light out. And then my aunt is coming to get me."

nine

"Your aunt? And who would that be?" Officer Lopez asks.

I tell them.

"She knows you're here?"

"Yes," I say. I show them the email from her.

"Right, well, how about we all wait for her back at the station? I think that's what we need to do," Sergeant Martin says. His partner closes my laptop and takes it.

Sergeant Martin takes my backpack while I'm putting on my coat.

Officer Lopez stops to talk to the counter woman. She must have been the one who called them.

And now they're going to take me back to that awful foster home.

I suddenly feel sick to my stomach. I grab the side of the police car, lean over and throw up on the ground. Sergeant Martin gets in the driver seat. Officer Lopez stands next to me. Then she opens the front seat, gets a bottle of water, twists off the top and hands it to me.

"Rinse out your mouth," she says. "Then spit!"

I do that.

She opens the back door, helps me in. Tells me to fasten the seatbelt. Closes the door.

I try to get the door open and make a run for it, while she's getting in next to me from the other side.

But I can't. The back-seat doors don't have any door

handles. You can't roll down the windows, either. Even if you could, they have bars on them. I guess once you're in here, you aren't ever getting out unless someone lets you out. It makes me very nervous, but there's nothing I can do. I'm trapped!

We start driving. The two officers don't talk, but they have a radio on and there's some talking on it. I can't quite hear it, but it's not like an ordinary radio. It sounds more like walkie-talkie messages but with a lot of static.

We pass more houses and stores. Turn onto a highway. Then off, passing more stores and businesses and finally, we turn into a parking lot next to a black building.

"Come on in, Sam!" Sergeant Martin says, holding the door open for me. "Place isn't fancy, but at least it's warm. And we'll figure out where you're supposed to be right now."

I have no choice but to follow him, with Officer Lopez right behind me. We get to a small room with just a table and four chairs. There's a computer that seems to be attached to the table.

"OK. Here's what's going to happen, Sam. You're going to tell us everything you can about how you got to be out alone in the middle of the night. Let's start with you tell me your full name and show me some ID, if you've got it. Anything with your name on it. And your picture. Got anything like that?"

I do. I reach into my backpack. Open the secret pocket. And pull out some papers and a little blue booklet.

nine

Hand them to Sergeant Martin.

"Oh," he says. "Well, this changes things."

He hands my passport and my middle school student card to Officer Lopez to look at.

"That's ID, isn't it? They've got my picture," I say. "And my name."

"Sure do," she says, sending her partner one of those adult looks.

Officer Martin is keying something into the computer. I can't see the screen, but I think I know what he's going to find. Charged for stealing. Children's custody. Another name for a jail, for kids. Like that horrible foster home. Only bigger. And you can't leave until you grow up.

I've read about them. Online.

"Tell me your parents' names. Addresses. Phone numbers."

I tell the officers my mother is on a plane. That we don't have an address anymore. Our house is sold. She's moving. To Hawaii.

"And you're supposed to be with her?"

I tell them about the airport. The two French women, in the washroom who wanted to steal my backpack.

"And you knew these women were speaking French – how?"

"*Parce-que Mademoiselle,*" I say, answering Officer Lopez, "*Je parle le français.*"

"Do you now?" she says, smiling. "So, what did these women in the bathroom have to say? And why didn't you just leave and get on your plane? With your mother?"

I tell them. Everything. I don't leave anything out. The women's names. Or at least the names I heard them call each other. What they said. Why I was in the ladies' for so long.

"And the airline didn't put you on the next plane out to join your mother?"

"Um, no. I didn't ask them. I didn't know I could. I thought I'd have to buy another ticket and..."

"I see. OK. Then what did you do?"

I tell them. Subway ride. Bus station. Bought two tickets to Boston. Emailed friends for help. I show the two officers my un-used bus tickets. They have the date and time when I bought the tickets printed on them.

"But you didn't send a message to your parents about this, uh, bus trip?"

"No."

"I wonder why. But we'll get to that. What happened next?"

Just wasting time, really, until it was time to get on the bus. Picked out a sandwich and a drink. Woman hit me and stepped on me. Man grabbed me. Police came and said I was a thief and I had to go and be searched and...

"Hold on a minute," he says. "I just want to be sure

nine

I'm hearing this right. Lopez, you getting all this?"

"Yes sir," she says.

They both ask some questions about details – who? When? Where? What did they look like? and I answer them.

"OK. Then what?"

The search. Going through my things. Taking my credit card. Finding things in my backpack that I didn't put there. The child custody woman. The foster home. The other kids there. Doreen and the baby. How I got my laptop back, but my phone is gone.

How I escaped. And ran and ran. And got to the donut store.

"Right," Sergeant Martin says when I pause and drink the last of my glass of water. "Do you have any idea where this place was?"

I tell him the street address of the house next door and that the peeling paint green house didn't have any number. "OK, very good," he says. "I'm on it, Steph. You carry on here."

"OK, Sam, you're doing great. So, can you describe the two, uh, people in police uniforms at the bus station?"

How tall they were. About how old. What colour hair. What kind of accent did they have. Any scars? Tatoos? Anything else about them I can remember.

I do that.

"Did you get names? Badge numbers? Anything like

that?"

No, I didn't. I describe their uniforms, different than the one Officer Lopez has.

"And the woman who drove you to the, uh, home?"

I describe her. Her car. But no, I didn't notice the license plate number. Why would I?

"And the woman there? Doreen? Anything more you can tell me about her?"

Her dirty long hair with gray roots. No make-up. Smudgy tattoos on her arms and legs. I try to think if there was anything else. But no, there's nothing more I can remember about her. Or that poor little smelly baby.

"But I'm worried about the other kids there."

I describe them. Everything I remember.

"Did you ever hear their names?"

"No. Not for the two boys. They mostly only talked to each other. And the little girl who cried but she wouldn't come with me. Her name is Rachelle. Rachelle Leitkov. And the other girl was Lakeesha. She was the one who kicked me. I don't know her last name."

"Kicked you? You didn't tell us this before."

I pull up my sweater and shirt. Most of my right side, from my chest down to my right thigh, is bluish-black with bruises.

"Oh my God," she says. "Why didn't you say sooner?"

nine

"I thought you were going to take me back to that place. The foster home."

"Listen to me, Sam. That wasn't a foster home. And those weren't real police officers, at the bus station. They are criminals. They were trying to kidnap you. And the other kids there."

"What? But why?"

"To get money. From your parents. To get you back."

"Like ransom money?" I say. There was something about that in my dad's movie.

"Yes, exactly like that. They wanted to hurt you. And your family." I start to feel shaky again. And sick. "But you're safe now."

Sergeant Martin comes back, signalling to Officer Lopez that he needs to talk to her. In private. That means so I can't hear what they say.

"OK, sweetheart. Do you think you could tell our artist so she can draw the people you've told us about?"

Yes, I think I can do that. Even though my eyes are just about closing themselves, I'm so sleepy. And I really need to use the washroom.

She comes there with me, waits while I use the toilet and wash my hands and face again, and then we walk through some doors and halls and more doors. Finally, we get to another desk. I tell the artist, Luca, what the two people who I thought were police officers at the bus station look like. Also, the woman who shoved into me and the man at the store, the ones who said I was stealing. And the tall woman who drove me to the place that isn't a foster home. And the big woman there, the one who took my laptop. But I got it back.

I remember them all pretty clearly, even though I wish I didn't. The scar the fake police officer woman had under her left eye. The purple streak the tall woman had in her black hair. The smudgy tattoos the big woman has. The only clear one looked like a skull and crossbones.

My throat is sore. It feels like I've talked and talked and talked.

Officer Lopez comes back to get me. She hands me a yogurt and a little spoon and some hot chocolate in a paper cup that is almost warm and a water bottle and a granola bar.

"Sorry," she says. "That's all there was in the machine. But the cafeteria should be open soon."

I sit down and peel the top off the yogurt. Peach flavour. Not my favourite, but I'm hungry so I don't care. I drink all the water and some of the hot chocolate.

Then I'm sleepy. I think I could fall asleep right here, in the police station, in this chair. But I can't. Not before I can find out what's going to happen next.

Where they're going to send me.

Or are they going to call Eira and Dom to come get me?

Or what?

"Just a couple more things we need to know," Sergeant Martin says. "We know your mother was on

nine

that plane but we've now learned there was an incident."

"What?" I say. "What does that mean? Did the plane crash?"

"No. No. Nothing like that," he says. "Just that your mother got into...an argument. On the plane. With another passenger and the flight attendants. Your mother's with the police now. In Honolulu."

"What does that mean?" I ask, thinking how bizarre is that, both of us are talking to police officers right now? And what could possibly happen on a plane that would mean my mother has to talk to the police? Unless she went there to tell them I'm missing?

"Right. So, Sam, you never did tell us your other details, like who is your father? Since we can't get your mother just now, we're going to have to call him."

"No!" I say, louder than I meant to. "I mean, um, you can't!"

"No? Why not?"

Good question. Why not?

"Well, because he doesn't live here. I mean, near here. He lives in California. With his other family."

"I see." Officer Lopez says, though I can tell she doesn't. Or maybe she thinks I'm lying. "Even so, I think we have to contact him. I need his name and phone number. You've got it there in your laptop, don't you?"

I hesitate.

"I can just take the laptop and find it, Sam. We have people here who can figure out how to get into your laptop in about 30 seconds. Or, you can just tell me."

I tell her.

"WHAT?" she says. "Sarg, get over here. You've got to hear this! Sam, tell him!"

I sigh. And do what she wants.

"Right," he says. "Well, that changes things some more, doesn't it?"

I don't know why it would. I just shrug, too tired to answer.

"And this aunt you say is coming for you? Who's she?"

I open my contacts file on my laptop and show them.

The officers say they have some work to do, and why don't I try to nap a bit while they do their jobs? Another officer will be right there at the door, they say. They'll find a pillow and blanket for me. I'll be totally safe.

I'm grateful to pull my coat around me, even though now it's pretty grubby, but there's also a nice clean blanket they give me. I close my eyes, wondering what will happen next. Though, right now, I'm almost too tired to care.

My face feels hot and it's throbbing around my right eye. My throat feels raw, like I need to cough but can't. My body hurts. My brain hurts. My right hand hurts.

My whole world hurts.

ten

I'm making a list. Not in writing. In my head.

It's a list of what I've got. And what I've lost.

This is on the 'got it' list:

The sweater, jeans and tee shirt that I just took off. My wet winter boots, socks and my jacket. These are all on a heap on the floor right now. I don't want to put any of them back on, not ever, but I guess I'll have to. Some of them, at least.

My laptop and its charging cable.

My headphones.

My passport.

My music ideas notebook.

My boarding pass to get on the plane to Hawaii that left without me.

My two bus tickets to get on the bus to Boston that

also left without me.

My student card.

Some money that was still hidden in the secret pocket. I count it. 52 dollars and 25 cents.

One almost-clean pair of jeans and, stuffed way down in the bottom, a pair of clean socks.

One pair of underwear and the frilly pink blouse my mother made me wear for my lesson with Madame and for the auditions.

One little cosmetic bag with my hairbrush, toothbrush and travel-size shampoo and toothpaste.

My chopsticks case with the red-for-good-luck chopsticks still inside.

All of this just came out of my backpack. Now it's spread out in front of me, on the bench in a white shower room. At the police station.

Officer Wang, but she says I can call her Naomi, is right outside the door till I come out. She says I'm totally safe. I can take as long as I want.

I want to take as little time as possible. This small white room with no window is too much like being trapped somewhere. In a white box.

I know I'm safe now. Or safe enough. At the police station with people who are real police. Not just actor thieves or whatever they were at the bus station. Which was also only yesterday.

So different from right now, when I'm wrapped in a towel in a small white shower room with every single

ten

thing I own in the world spread out on the bench. I'm looking at what I've got. And thinking about all that's missing.

My velvet skirt and tights, that go with the dress-up blouse. My good shoes, the ones I like to wear when I perform.

My favourite tee shirt, the aqua one with long sleeves.

My swimsuit, for just in case the hotel we stay at has a pool.

My phone. My credit cards. My pajamas and nightgown. The earrings and wish bracelet Morley made for me. When did I lose them?

I don't know.

And there are the bigger things that are gone. Much bigger.

My piano. My bedroom, in my home. In my town. My friends…pretty much everything important.

But I can't let myself think about them, or I'll just cry. Again.

Instead, I have to brush my hair back. Not look too closely in the mirror, because now the bruises on my face are darker than they were. They're achy, but not near as bad as they look. Same with the ones on my chest and down my right side.

I get dressed. Put the dirty clothes and the rest of my stuff back in my backpack.

Open the door. Thank Naomi for waiting for me and follow her down the hall, wondering where we're going. And what will happen next.

Will Umma get back on another plane and get me? If so, then what?

Or will my Dad come? But, if he does, wouldn't I have to go live with his new family in California? I already know how much his wife doesn't want that and I sure don't, either.

Or, what? Would they send me to a foster home? I mean an actual one, for orphans or homeless kids. Is that what I am, now?

"Come on," Naomi says, still leading me through doors and along hallways. "You want some breakfast? We're going to stop off at the canteen." We do that. I get chocolate milk, a banana and a little package of cookies, just to keep her happy. I'm more nervous than hungry, just wondering what's going to happen next. I wish she'd tell me. But no, she says, checking her phone again before saying that Officer Lopez and Sergeant Martin will be in soon. They've got some news.

"Is it good news?"

She won't say. "Best to hear it when we get back to the squad room," is all she'll tell me.

We go through the last set of doors and into a big open room where there are phones ringing, officers and people who don't wear uniforms walking around, talking, working on computers, sipping coffee or tea from paper cups, and...

"EIRA," I scream, running into her arms. "Aunt Eira, you came!"

ten

"Well, um, not exactly aunt…" Dom, now right behind her, is saying.

"Stop that," Eira says, laughing. I don't know if she means Dom or me. "How are you, darling? We heard you were hurt. Oh dear, your face…"

"I'm better. Now you're here," I say. "But are you…"

I mean to say "Are you going to take me to the airport and put me on the plane to Hawaii?" but before I can say this, Officer Lopez and Sergeant Martin are there, and suddenly everyone in the room is standing and clapping, like it's right after some incredible performance.

I don't understand. But I can't find out, because the two police officers say we need to go someplace a bit quieter. They lead us to what looks like a small living room. Everything in it is gray or cream-coloured. There are sofas and chairs. But nothing on the walls. And no windows.

"OK, there is good news. And some not-so-good news," Stephanie Lopez says. "Sam, it's up to you. Which do you want to start with?"

I'm sitting between Dom and Eira on the couch. Eira is holding my hand. Dom is holding my backpack and jacket. Good or bad? I shrug. "I've had a lot of bad lately," I say. "So maybe start with the good?"

"Fair enough," Officer Lopez says. "The good is we've heard from your father and, I believe, so has your aunt here."

Oh no, I think. How could this be good?

"He can't come right away to be with you. But he has sent word that you are to go with your Aunt Eira and Mr. Andreescu here. He's sent you a voice message. Shall I play it for you?"

What? I'm so confused. I'm to go with Eira and Dom. To California? I don't get it.

Officer Lopez pulls out her phone, thumbs to a message and we all listen as my father says, "This is Deveraux Lewis. I am the biological father of Sam Hae Park and share custody of our daughter with her mother, Soo Min Park. While her mother is detained in Hawaii and I am unable to come to New York right now, I have had my lawyer draw up a temporary guardianship document.

"It is my understanding that Ms. Star and Mr. Andreescu have seen this document, signed it with their lawyer today and all is in proper order for Ms. Star and Mr. Andreescu to take my daughter Sam Park back to their home in Seabright, with my full approval.

"Sam, these are good people. I know you spent Christmas with them, you have known Ms. Star and her family for several years and you will be safe with them and, I hope, happy. I can add that I have assurances both about them and from them that you will receive excellent care. To help with this, the amount that normally goes to your mother each month for your upkeep will now be sent to Ms. Star. This will continue to pay for your music lessons as well as all your other expenses.

"Sam, from what I am told, you have had a difficult

few days. But now you are safe, you are with good people who care about you, and I will see you as soon as I am able to get away."

There is a pause, and then it seems everyone is talking.

Except me.

I can't take it in.

Eira hugs me. "Sam, do you understand?" she says. "You're coming home with us."

Home, I think. With Eira. And Dom.

"For how long?" Will they just let me stay there for, like a few days, or a few weeks? Then I have to go somewhere else?

"For now. That's all we're worried about."

"Is that the bad news?"

Officer Lopez, who had been grinning, looks more serious.

Eira moves closer and puts an arm around me. I guess she already knows what he's going to say.

"It's about your mother," he says. "Something happened. On the way to Hawaii."

"Is she all right? She's not hurt, is she…?"

"No. no, nothing like that," he says. "It's just that she became…upset I guess you could call it … on the plane."

Yes, I can picture her doing that.

"She slapped a cabin crew member and kicked another passenger. This means she was taken into custody when the plane landed in Honolulu. At that point, it seems she assaulted a police officer, though of course that is unproven."

My mother got angry and attacked some people? Really? Why?

"Has Ms. Park been arrested?" Dom asks.

"She has been sent for a psychological assessment," Sergeant Martin says. "Depending on what that result is, she could be charged. If that happens, she could then be released on bail. Or held, as a flight risk. Sam, do you understand what this means?"

"Finding out if she's got a mental illness? Or she was just really angry and hit them and she gets arrested? If that happens, she could be let out of jail or have to stay there?"

"Yes, that pretty much sums it up. Does this upset you? Or surprise you?"

Not really, no. I tell them about the pills she takes and all the wine she drinks. About the online gambling games I saw her playing. About all the times she left me in hotel rooms and was gone for hours and hours. And about how she's either really angry all the time, or really kind of happy and dreamy.

They exchange looks. The kind of looks adults do that mean it's serious and we'll talk about it later when kids can't hear.

"I think she might be an addict," I say, seeing the shocked looks on the four adult faces.

ten

"What would make you say this?" Officer Lopez says, at the same time that Eira says, "What? Really?"

So, I tell them. I looked it up, online, about addiction. I know it's different, in women, than it is for men, and why. I tell them everything I've seen my mother do, everything she's said that I remember, everything that happened ever since she picked me up at Morley's house after Christmas.

And some of the things before that. Like selling our home and making it a secret.

Everyone is listening, except for Officer Lopez. Stephanie. She's recording what I'm saying and also taking notes.

"We do know that your mother left her job. Back in November," she says.

"Because she got a new job in Hawaii," I say. "That's what she said."

"Uh, no. At least, not that we can discover. She left her former employer. She was asked to leave."

"What?" Eira says. "She was fired? Do you know why?"

"Not yet, no. And it might not be relevant. But we do know that she had plans to meet a Mr. Phillip James on arrival at Honolulu airport. My colleague there tells me that they did look for this gentleman, but it appears that..."

"He doesn't exist," Dom says. "He promised her all sorts of things, after she sent him money..."

"Yes, it appears that's what happened."

"Will he be charged?"

"No idea. Possibly. If they can find him."

"But what about Umma?" I say. "Will they let her go soon?"

"I don't think so, Sam. It doesn't work that way. We've now learned she's under a 30-day Observation Order. That means she has to stay where she is, for now."

"Where?"

"At a secure facility. It's a sort of hospital. Bit nicer than a jail, usually. But once you're there, you're not allowed to leave. Though you can have visitors, if you and your Aunt and Uncle here want to take you there to see her?"

"No, I don't think so. I mean no, I don't want to go," I say. "But I do hope she gets better." It doesn't sound like a place she'd like to be. Or anyone would want to be at.

"At which point, she could be charged. More likely, the charges will be dropped. It seems the company she worked for would rather keep this hushed up. I understand she was a lawyer at that company, is that right?"

"Yes," I say. They already know this, don't they?

"But she probably won't be allowed to practice law, not after this," Sergeant Martin says.

"Because she hit some people on the plane? And then the police officer?"

ten

"Well, that's bad enough. But her main problem is that, where she used to work, there is some money missing. Quite a lot of money, it turns out. All belonging to her clients."

Oh. That's bad. Really bad.

"She's a thief?"

"Possibly. Nothing is proven. We don't know if her former employer will be pressing charges."

"But if they do?"

"She could be brought back from Hawaii to face charges. If it comes to that."

My father is in California. But he said I can live with Eira and Dom. For now.

My mother is arrested. In Hawaii. And she's in big trouble. For hitting people. And, maybe, stealing a lot of money.

It's…I don't know what it is. Unbelievable. Crazy.

Like something you see on TV.

Or in one of my dad's movies. Although usually they don't have any kids in them.

Not like things that happen in real life.

"It's a lot to try to take in," Officer Lopez says. "You're a brave girl, though. Strong and smart. We know this. You got away from the bad guys. And you gave us really good descriptions of them so there's a good chance they'll be caught."

I hope so.

"Will Sam...will we have to come back? I mean, if you find those people? If there's a trial?" Eira asks.

"We can't really say, at this point, though it seems unlikely."

"And have you found them?" I ask. "Have you found Rachelle? And Lakeesha? And the two boys?"

"Not yet, no. We're doing everything we can to get them back safe," Sergeant Martin says.

"Will you let me know? I mean, when they're safe?"

"We will," the officers say, standing and shaking hands with Dom, then Eira and finally, me. "We'll stay in touch."

"Thank you," I say, hugging each of the officers. "Thank you for helping them and saving me."

And then we're out in the car. Driving back to the airport.

On our way home, to my old new home. Or my new old home. In Seabright.

eleven

Way back last summer when my best friends and I made wish bracelets, the wish for mine was that I could always live in Seabright. It's my home and the place I love. Where my friends are. Where my music is. Where my heart is, as Madame says.

Now, finally, my bracelet wish has come true!

AND I got my Christmas wish, the one that Jayden, Morley and I made in December. It was just to have a Christmas. Just once.

A real Christmas. Not just all the getting-to-Christmas kinds of things we do at school, or going to the Santa Claus parade in the city, or buying a toy for the Wish Tree at the mall, or the way people decorate their houses.

I did get a real Christmas with my friends, the Star family.

As if all that wasn't lucky enough, now I've got my piano back. Or I'll have it soon. The people who bought our house decided they didn't even want it. They were going to sell it to their friends! When Dom found that out, he offered them more money to sell it to us, along with some other things left behind in our house that I still wanted, like my bed and desk. And Margaret's red couch, where we watched movies together.

But I didn't get all these things right away. That's because Eira pointed out that there just isn't room for everything in her little condo. It had plenty of space for just her and Dom and Pixel, but wasn't big enough for all of us now, including someone who owns a grand piano.

So we went house-hunting. That's what Eira calls it. It means you look at houses that are for sale and pick one. I love the place we found. It isn't really big and fancy, like my old home was. It's more of a bungalow, something the real estate man called "ranch style." It is all on one floor, but with lots of space including a TV room and a garden. There's also a big garage and workshop which Dom says is going to be his man-cave. And a granny suite, that's sort of a little apartment that Eira says maybe we'll rent out to a student or someone to be here and look after Pixel when we go on our skiing vacation next month.

Or, and this is a big surprise that they just told me about, back to France this summer. Madame has invited me to her music school for all of July and August, if I want to come. I can't wait!

At the same time, Eira and Dom are going to do

eleven

something Eira says she's always wanted to do, which is live in Europe for a summer. She says she might even try to learn to speak French or Spanish, like I do!

When I got back to Seabright, I had some thank you notes to write. To Police Constable Lopez. To her colleague, Sergeant Martin. I even sent one to the donut shop, to the woman there who called the officers, even though I couldn't remember her name. I hope she got it.

I went back to school. And back to my new education plan. It turned out I only missed a week or so of classes.

Lots of people wanted to know where I'd been. I just said on vacation, in New York City, with my mum. "Oh, cool," they said. "Lucky you!"

I just smile and say, "Yeah, I am! And how was your Christmas?"

I told Morley and Jayden more about what happened. Not all of it. There are just some things I really need to think about and try to figure out on my own. And also with Eira. She is so good at just listening. She never judges, like Umma did. She just nods.

She says it's OK to be afraid. To run, when you're scared. Sometimes, she says, running is the smartest thing you can do.

She says we all mistakes. That's just what humans do. We make mistakes so we figure out what went wrong, and fix it. As much as we can.

She says Umma has certainly made some mistakes. We still don't know all of what happened and probably never will.

I say I feel sorry for her. Even though she hurt me. She really wasn't a very good mother.

No, Eira says, in a lot of ways, she wasn't. But in some ways maybe she was. "I know you're angry at her now. You have every right to be angry. But do you think maybe, someday, you'll be able to understand what she did? Try to forgive her?"

I don't know. Maybe. "Why would I?"

"Because staying angry isn't good, ever. Letting go of being angry isn't for her, it's for you. It will help you feel better," Eira says. "Let's try to think about the positive things. Like what she gave you."

What she gave me? Mostly, she ignored me. Or bullied me into always working harder. And then she took my whole life away.

"She hurt me," I say now. "She left me."

"Yes, she did. But we also need to look at what she gave you. Your home. Here in Seabright."

"But then she just sold it. Because of gambling and losing all that money. And then she gambled some more and lost the house money, too."

"Yes. It appears that way. But let's stay positive here. What else did she give you?"

"I don't know. What?" I want to stay mad at my mother. I want to hate her, for what she did. She deserted me in the airport. She didn't care enough about me to make sure I was with her and safe, on the plane.

eleven

The plane I refused to get on.

"Well, music lessons, for one. She made sure you got the best teachers. The best opportunities," Eira says.

"Which my Dad paid for. Mostly."

"True. But your mother made it happen. And encouraged you…"

Ordered me around. Didn't listen. Bossed and nagged me, mostly. Had a bunch of stupid rules.

"…to take advantage of those lessons and opportunities. With Anton and Sonya, and Madame…"

"Yeah. I guess."

"And another thing she gave you. A stable home. With Margaret."

"Who's gone now. Because of her!" I say, "and I'm never going to see her again!"

"Don't be so sure," Eira says, looking out the living room window of her condo, where we've been sitting on the couch. For some reason, she's grinning.

I have to know why. I go over to the window and see a taxi pulling up out front. A short woman, all bundled up in a long puffy coat and a lot of scarves, gets out. A woman who looks very familiar. But it's can't be!

She's holding an overstuffed tote bag and a big purse. She turns and…

YES! IT'S MARGARET!

twelve

For a moment she stands there, as if she's not sure if this is the right address.

I'm so excited to see her, I don't even stop to pull on my boots or grab my coat. I run down the stairs and outside and into Margaret's arms, just as the taxi is pulling away.

"*Mi corazón*," she says, laughing. "But you get so cold in only slippers. No coat. Inside now, hurry!"

There are a million things I want to ask her. And tell her. I hardly know where to begin.

Yes, her Christmas at home with her family was wonderful, Margaret says as Eira hands her a cup of tea and I pass the plate that I've just loaded up with brownies. Her mother is well, or as well as she can be, with her arthritis and all. Her kids are all great, excellent. One of her daughters has just started training to be a nurse. Her son plays guitar and is crazy about soccer. Her other daughter has left school

twelve

because she got a job in an office.

Margaret wants to know about how Mrs. Park is doing. My mother. And is she enjoying Hawaii, as she thought she would?

"Yes. I guess so," I say though the truth is, I don't know. The only messages I've gotten from her were emails about how everything was my fault and if I'd just gotten on the plane, like I was supposed to, none of this would have happened.

She didn't even ask how I was and what happened, after she got on that plane without me.

I wrote back saying that I was staying at Eira's and Dom's now and hoped she was feeling better soon.

She just wrote back with another it's-all-your-fault-Sam message.

I didn't bother answering.

Margaret asks about Umma. How she likes Hawaii? Or is she headed back here already?

"We don't really know," Eira says. "She's probably just, uh, trying to deal with being where she is. I mean, getting settled down there. In Hawaii."

I stare at her. This is only sort-of true. Eira isn't going to tell Margaret the real truth? I wonder why not.

"But we're delighted to have Sam with us, while her parents are, um, sorting things out. Between them."

An adult look passes between them. It makes me wonder what Eira and Dom aren't telling me.

Or maybe just don't want to discuss, in front of me.

"But tell me, Margaret, you're comfortable at my sister's?" Eira says.

What? Margaret is staying at Sorcha's? Does that mean she's going to work for them now, taking care of their twins? Sorcha is Morley's other aunt and the twins are her cousins.

I can't stop myself interrupting to ask. But I've got it all wrong. Margaret isn't looking after Sorcha's kids. She's staying at Morley's!

"Yes, very comfortable, Senorita Star," Margaret says. "Thank you so much for making this arrangement. I have some of my things there now. Other things in storage, come from Señora Park house you know, I go and get them soon."

"Yes, of course. Dom and I will help you. Sam too," Eira says. "When do you want to do that?"

They talk about days and times. It seems that Margaret is staying at the bed-and-breakfast Morley and her mother run, in Seabright. She helps with the new baby, Lily, in the mornings and cooks and cleans for them. Then she'll come here in the afternoons and pick me up after school. Sundays are her day off. Just like always.

I can hardly believe it! Margaret is back AND I'll get to see her almost every day!

"Yes, excellent," Eira says. "I'm so pleased you could come back. Helping out Eefa right now and for Sam and for us!"

"For time being," Margaret adds.

twelve

For the time being? Does that mean for not very long? Like, just a visit?

I must look really upset, because Eira says, "Here's what we haven't told you yet, Sam. You already know we're going to buy a new house, bigger than here. So, until we move into our new home, Margaret is staying at Morley's place."

"And then what?"

"Well, we'll get a place that's big enough for all of us. With an apartment for Margaret so she can look after us."

I'm confused. "But I thought you had a new job? With a different family?"

Margaret just shrugs. "No more," she says. "Much better here, with you and Star family. In Seabright."

I know exactly what she means.

~ ~ ~

It's the week of March break when Eira, Dom, Margaret and I move into our new house. It isn't the largest one we looked at, or the really small one that was right on the ocean, or the old captain's house out in the country, near Jayden's. There were good things about all of them, but just one that looked like it would suit everyone. That's the one Eira and Dom bought.

Eira fell in love with the garden. Dom went nuts for

the garage-workshop, his new man-cave. Margaret was really pleased about the granny suite, where she gets a garden view and also her own tiny but private patio. I love it that the living room has a huge bay window, the perfect spot for my piano.

I got to paint my bedroom any colour I wanted, so now it's green and I love it. Even with things from our old house and Eira's condo and Dom's old apartment, our home now looks so different than any of them. Maybe because Eira and her sister Eefa just have this talent for mixing colours and making any room look comfortable and interesting. Like a place you really want to be and where you can relax. It's that way at Morley's. And now it's like that at our house.

Morley gave me a Welcome Home present of some bedsheets with music notes all over them and a pretty aqua and green duvet. Daisy and Gus made some birdfeeders to hang on the big maple tree in our new back yard. Jayden and Morley framed three funny photos Jayden took of Tippy during his doggie vacation and helped me hang them up in my bedroom.

Margaret, Dom and I hauled a lot of boxes out of the storage locker. They all had Umma's name and mine on them, but Margaret still had the storage locker key. We paid off the storage people and brought everything home. It was like having another Christmas, opening all those boxes and pulling out our clothes and books and other stuff, like some of Margaret's favourite cookware.

It just felt so good to have our own stuff again. It makes this house feel even more like our home.

twelve

My only worry is, for how long?

What if my father changes his mind, about Eira and Dom being my temporary guardians?

What does temporary mean? How long does it last for?

What if Umma comes back and says I have to go live with her somewhere?

I don't talk about any of this with Morley and Jayden. I just don't think they'd understand. Jayden has both his parents around. Always has. Even if his dad is kind of strict and grumpy and his mom is always so busy, with being a vet and everything. Plus Jayden is the youngest kid in his family. He says that usually means you get forgotten in the crowd.

And Morley doesn't have her father. She's never even met him. But she's lived with her mother all her life. And had her aunts, Eira and Sorcha, really close. And now Dom, who is going to be her new uncle because he and Eira are getting married in June.

Which, they say, is another good reason for buying the house and getting moved in. It means they already have all that moving work done so they can just enjoy their wedding. And then their honeymoon to France.

In February, Dom and Eira were going to go on a skiing vacation, just the two of them. A romantic getaway, Dom called it. I figured I'd just stay home while they were gone, or maybe if Margaret also wanted to go away for a break I'd stay at Morley's place. That would be OK. Her new baby sister, Lily, is a sweetheart. I like giving her a bottle and even learned how to make her burp after feeding and change her diaper. I've always wondered what it would be like to have a brother. Or a sister. Lucky Morley, she's got two sisters. But Jayden is even luckier, he's got five brothers!

But no staying home for me. Dom got the tickets changed and I got to go with them. To Whistler Ski Resort. That's out West in the Rocky Mountains. Skiing is something I never had a chance to do before, but I have seen pictures of families skiing. It's even more fun than it looks like, even if you're not very good at it, like me, and you fall a lot. There were lots of kids, and even some grown-ups like Dom, on the bunny hills.

That's what they call it, if you're a beginner.

Eira is a great skier, so we hardly saw her except in the evenings. She said next year, when we go back, I should be tall enough to go on the sky-way lift. That is, if I get better enough at downhill skiing for the bigger runs.

Dom decided skiing isn't for him. But he just loves snowboarding.

We'd hardly moved into our new house and there were still boxes everywhere, when there was a knock at the front door.

Margaret was out visiting a friend and Eira and I were unpacking dishes, washing them and putting them away, so Dom went to answer the door.

Dom came back into the kitchen a minute later, with

twelve

someone behind him.

"DAD!" I shout. "But how did you know...?"

"Hey, kiddo!" he says, stopping to kiss me on the cheek. "How ya doin'?"

Dom gets two beers from the fridge, hands one to my father and leads the way to the living room. Eira grabs a cloth to dry her hands.

"Looks like a good place you got here," Dad says. "Happy with it?"

"Very," Eira says. "We were lucky. The people who had it wanted to downsize and they were in a hurry to get into their new place, so it all just worked out!"

"And I understand you've got Margaret with you?"

I didn't even think my Dad knew about Margaret. Or anything about our lives, in Seabright. I guess I was wrong.

The adults chat for a while. About dumb things, like the weather. How my Dad missed his connecting flight and it took so long to get here. And he's not used to snow.

"Nobody ever is," Dom jokes. "But you sure you're dressed for it? I could lend you a warmer coat, if you want."

"No, I'm OK," Dad says. "Can't stay that long. I fly out again tonight. On the red-eye."

Oh. So it's going to be a short visit. Which makes me wonder why he's here.

"I want to say a few things to all three of you. But

first, let me have some time with Sam. There are some things she needs to know. And I think she deserves an explanation."

"Of course," Eira says. "Come on, babe. You can help me finish up in the kitchen."

And then it's just the two of us. I wonder what kind of news my Dad has. And if it's good news.

He says he's sorry. He knows he hasn't been a very good father. Not around much, or in my life, even though that's what my mother wanted.

Really? I always thought she wanted to be with him, be his wife and we would be a family.

He says he'll try to do better. See me more often. At least a few times a year, he says, when he can get away.

"Get away from making movies?"

"Yes. From work."

"And from your other family?"

He sighs. "Look, Sam. You are my daughter. And they are also my daughter and my sons and my wife. I live with them. But I care about all of you. Love you all."

"Do you care about them more? Is that why you're with them?"

"It's not like that. It's just that me and your mother...well, it never really worked out between us."

"But you were married. And then you left us."

He looks shocked. "No, Sam. Your mother and I were

twelve

never married. Never even lived together. We went out a few times, that's all."

That isn't what Umma told me.

"So, it was just like boyfriend and girlfriend?"

"Not even that, I'm afraid. I'm sorry, sweetheart. It was just…"

"Just a mistake. You're saying I was just a mistake."

"No, I'm not saying that. A bit unexpected, maybe. Not a mistake. Not ever. I know your mother is very proud of you. We both are."

"But it would have been easier if, well if I never happened."

He looks down at his feet for a minute, as if a good answer might be printed on his socks because he left his shoes at the door.

"Look, I'm not good with the words like your mother is. But let me just say this, Sam. You are a gift. To your mother. To me. Maybe we haven't been much good at being your parents or telling you this, but we do care about you. Very much. Love you. Want the very best for you.

"And these people you're living with now, Eira and Dom, they're good people. The best. I know they care about you, too."

"How can you know that?" I shout. "How could you possibly know that, all the way out west in California? With your real family?"

"You're as real to me as they are. Haven't I always

supported you? So maybe I wasn't there, in person, to clean up after you and teach you how to throw a baseball and ride a bike and cheer for you at swimming races and concerts.

"But hey, you know what? I've always been there. Tried to see you, when I could. Had you come to stay, but you told me you didn't want to live with us out West. I understand that, even though it wasn't what I wanted. I did what I could for you. The music lessons, the big house, going to Paris. Sam, I knew about all that because I paid for it."

I'm so shocked I can't speak. It feels like there is a big clump of seaweed in my throat. It's like I want to choke. I can hardly breathe.

"And I had them checked out, Dom and Eira. And Margaret. You don't think I'd trust my daughter with total strangers, do you?"

"What does checked out mean?"

"I hired someone to look into their backgrounds. Be sure they're who they say they are."

"You had them investigated?" I say. "Like they were criminals, or something?"

"Nothing like that. But you have to know, Sam, I never make any kind of a deal without knowing who I'm dealing with."

"And I was just a deal? That's all?"

"Sam, take a deep breath. Think, for a minute. I know you're a smart kid. Now, would you trust something that is important to you to people you don't know at

twelve

all?"

I breathe.

Think.

No. Probably not.

"No. I know you wouldn't. I'm just doing the same. Making sure you're protected and safe. Because that's what I want for you. A good home…"

"Even if it's not with you."

"Yes," he says. "Even then. Because I'm still your dad. Always will be. Even if you're angry with me. And, let me tell you, you're going to be a teenager soon, which will give you plenty to be angry with me about. Or so they tell me, since you're my oldest kid, I haven't faced that. Yet."

"But," I say, "maybe you could make a movie about it?"

"That might be an idea," he says, smiling. "But there's something else, something serious, I have to tell you. Maybe we should ask your, um…Eira and Dom to come back so they can hear this, too."

He goes to call them while I think about what he said. Try to take it all in.

It isn't about my future. It seems that as long as I'm happy, I'll be living with Dom and Eira. Until I'm ready to go off to university or move out because I've grown up, because they'll be my official guardians, in addition to my dad.

"But what about Umma?" I ask as Dom and Eira come

in with worried looks and sit down.

My dad gets a pained look on his face. "Well, that's the news I have for you. It seems she's disappeared from that hospital place they had her at out in Honolulu."

"What? Disappeared?" Eira is saying what I'm thinking. "But how? Why?"

"She somehow finagled a day-visit pass from one of the doctors. Family members came to collect her and then..."

"She didn't come back," Dom says. "The family scooped her."

"Seems like," Dad says. "Straight to the airport. Their private jet was waiting. They went back to South Korea. Who knows how they got the clearances, but I take it the Parks are a pretty powerful family, back in Busan. She left with just the clothes she was wearing. No phone, no laptop, not even her passport which the police had taken from her."

"But what does that mean? If that's what's happened?"

"Don't know. But she'd have trouble coming back here. Would probably be arrested if she tried."

"But what if that didn't happen? What if she got kidnapped or something? By criminals?"

Like I did.

"It doesn't look like that happened, because there was a message. From her. After. Saying that it was her choice to go home to be with her family in South

twelve

Korea. And not to try to trace her."

Oh. She's left her home, left her job, left everything. Including me. But maybe it wasn't her choice. Maybe her family made her go back with them.

"But you did try, didn't you?" Dom asks.

Dad laughs. "Of course I did. You don't think I'd let things end like that? For one thing, what would I say to Sam?"

I don't know. What would he say? What could anyone say? It was like something out of a movie. Or a TV show. Too strange to be real.

"So, what did your investigator find out?" Eira asks.

"Quite a bit, as it turns out. Though some of this, a lot of this, has to remain in this room. Between the four of us."

"And your guy? You can trust him?" Dom says.

"Absolutely. As much as I trust you three," Dad says.

"Officially, Soo Min Park is missing. Unofficially, she's back in Busan." He pulls out his phone and displays a photo. It's kind of fuzzy, but you can tell it's Umma, walking in a park with two men. They look a lot the same but one of them is older. "That's your grandfather, Sam. You mom's father, Park Ki-ja. And this guy is your Uncle Park Jang-ja."

"Do you know where they live? How to contact them?"

"Yep. And I'll leave that with you. And look, I've got the driver waiting outside in 20 minutes and there's more you need to know."

"How about you just talk, and we listen?" Dom says.

Dad nods. "OK, here's the story. You know Soo Min had some trouble at work…"

We all nod yes.

"…that was back in the fall. She left, well, she was told to leave…"

"Fired?"

"Yes. That's confirmed. There was money missing. Clients unhappy."

"And the money was for gambling," I say.

Three surprised adult faces turn my way.

"You knew?"

"I was pretty sure, yes."

"But you never said anything. Like to Margaret. Or me."

"You weren't around. And how could I tell Margaret? What could she have done about it? Umma was her boss."

"Good point," Dad says. "I knew you were a smart girl!"

His investigator found that not only did my mother take more than $300,000 from clients and lose it gambling, she also had debts. A lot of debts. That's why she had to sell our home. And her apartment in the city. Even with that, she was bankrupt. And there were some dangerous people she owed money to. That means she had no money left, owed a lot of

twelve

money, had no job and was in serious trouble. Which was also why she needed to get away. As far away as possible.

"Seems like she thought she could outrun all the people she owed money to in Hawaii," my Dad says. "It might have worked, but not for long."

When Margaret left for Mexico, she hadn't been paid for two months. It was my Dad who sent her the money Umma owed her. My mother was also behind in paying Sonya and Anton for my music lessons. And she owed a lot of money to the government for taxes she hadn't paid.

"So, she was in a really terrible situation," Eira says. "Poor woman. She must have been under terrible stress. No wonder she had a breakdown."

"Money problems. Gambling. And there's more," Dad says. "There were drugs found. Cocaine, mostly but also Ecstasy and some illegal painkillers. Fentanyl. Not in her bags but sewn into the lining of Sam's suitcase."

"Oh, no!" Eira says. "But if Sam had gotten on that plane with her…where would she be now?"

"That could have been…difficult," my Dad says grimly. "But we would have got you back, sweetheart. Don't worry."

"As it was, it was bad enough," Eira says. "Dom and I were so worried. I'm sure Sam was terrified."

"But very brave," my Dad says. "Smart and brave. That's our girl!"

Then, too soon, there's a knock on the door. It's Dad's driver, saying they better get going. There's another storm on the way, coming up the coast. Flights are still arriving and leaving, but maybe not for much longer.

My Dad's given us all the contact information for him, for his assistant who can always reach him and also for my mother's family in South Korea. Busan. That's the city they live in. I have to look it up online to figure out where it is.

And wonder if I'll ever go there. To meet my other family. My Asian family.

thirteen

Maybe my mother wants to talk to me, but she can't.

Maybe her new phone doesn't work to call to another country that's so far away. Even further than Hawaii.

Maybe she doesn't have her own laptop anymore. Or a computer. Or any way to text or message me. Even though she wants to. She did send me those two messages. But that was when she was still in Hawaii.

Maybe I should try to call her. I'm pretty sure that's possible. We might be able to set up an online video chat. Just so I could know she's OK and she likes being back in her home in Korea. That investigator my dad hired probably has a phone number for someone in the Park family.

Maybe I'll just send another email to her, after school. When I'm supposed to be practicing. Getting ready for my lesson tomorrow with Sonja. Because, lucky for me, she and Anton have both welcomed me back as their student.

Or maybe I won't. It could be that Eira is right about maybe my mother and I just need a time out. To think things through, for me. And for my mother to get better.

Eira explained about how she has a friend who's a therapist who works with people with addictions. She said that it's pretty common for people who have an addiction to one thing, like say using cocaine or shoplifting or alcohol to also have another addiction, like Umma does with gambling. They just can't stop, even when they know it's destroying their lives and hurting other people.

How did it hurt others? Well, she stole a lot of money, so it hurt the people who trusted her. That's probably also true about the people she worked with. They must have trusted her and been let down.

She hurt Margaret, who depended on her job with our family, because Margaret sends most of her money home to support her mother and her kids.

She hurt me. She never really trusted me. Never treated me with any kind of respect or caring. I can't remember one single time my mother ever hugged me, or kissed me, or said one kind thing to me. I can't remember her ever wanting to know about what I was thinking and feeling. It was like she thought I was just a music robot.

But Margaret did all those things I wanted my mother to do. I guess you could say in almost all the ways that matter, Tia Margaret is my real mother. She's the one who always was there. Always listened. Always cared about me, Sam Park, the real person. Not just

thirteen

Sam Park the musician.

I'm so lucky to have her back in my life. And to have Eira and Dom, who really didn't expect to have an instant family, even before they got married. When you think about it, it's a pretty special thing they're doing, giving me a home. And more than that. All the listening to me, and hugs, and just general kindness any one girl can cope with!

Just kidding. They're great. I'm so lucky.

And, you know, I don't think any of it could have happened if there hadn't been my accidental Christmas!

fourteen

It was April when we found out that the police in New York had arrested most of the people they think were involved in the kidnapping ring. They got the woman with the dirty baby and also the woman who was at the bus station shop and barged into me. They found Lakeesha and the two boys, but Rachelle is still missing. Officer Lopez said I was the only one they know of who managed to escape on my own.

I wish I'd not bothered about getting my laptop, even though it did have the concerto I was writing on it. I should have backed up my music on a memory stick. I should have just left the laptop there. I should have grabbed Rachelle. Made her come with me. I should have saved her.

That's not the only thing I should have done. But we all make mistakes, Eira says. That's just being human. It's also how we learn. And grow.

Eira and Dom took me to the city, to pick out another

violin. It was a friend of Anton's who was selling it and Anton said he knew it's a good instrument, so we got it.

It was a surprise when, one day in April, a courier driver knocked at our door. She said she needed a signature from Mr. Sam Park. I said it's me and signed for it. She handed me a box that turned out to be my old violin.

Inside was a note. It seems the cabin crew found it at Honolulu airport, when they were tidying up to get ready for boarding to head back to Los Angeles. One of them turned it in to their lost and found, where it sat for a while before someone looked inside, found my name and address and sent it back to our old home.

The people there told the driver our new address. Now that I don't need it, it came all the way back to me. But I'm happy to have it.

I'm happy, full stop. That's what I said in my thank-you notes.

There's so much to be happy about. Margaret likes our new home. She's excited about her mom and kids coming to visit soon. They'll be here for what's really exciting, Eira's and Dom's wedding.

Dad and his wife are invited. He says he doesn't know, but he'll try to make it.

My mother won't. I tried to stay angry with her, but the anger just turned into mostly sadness. I'm sad for her. I think she never really got what she wanted, which was to be a famous opera singer, but no one helped Umma get her dream. I'm not sure about this but I think that maybe no one loved her enough.

Or maybe she just never learned how to love herself. I mean, in the good way that gives you strength and confidence. One thing I've learned is that you can be the world's best at something, but if you don't have confidence, no one will ever know it. And it will never give you joy.

I'm so much more fortunate. I have my good friends, Morley and Jayden. I have my teachers, Anton and Sonja and Madame Boulanger. And Monsieur Cadeau. I have my dad, not exactly in my life, but not out of it, either. I know he cares about me. Loves me.

I have the generosity and kindness of Eira and Dom, who've given me a new home and a real family. And, best of all, I have my dear Tia Margaret. And I have Tippy.

Margaret says some people just aren't any good at loving. It's something you need to learn how to do. Some people never learn. Or they never get the chance. Or they throw away all their chances.

She doesn't say who she means by some people. I know she doesn't mean herself. Or me. Perhaps she means Umma.

Eira says family are the people you choose to have in your life. To love. To cherish. They aren't always the people you were born to.

I guess that's right. After all, look at Eira and Dom. And me. They chose each other. And they chose to have me in their family. I choose to have them.

fourteen

And Gus. Morley chose to have him in her family.

And Margaret. I know now that she's always been my family.

And Madame Boulanger. It's true, my mother paid her money to give me master classes in violin and piano. But there are way more people who want classes with Madame than she has time to teach and help. She chose me.

Maybe being related by love is stronger than being related by blood. Just like Margaret says.

Something that worried me is: What if my mother comes back? What if I have to go back to living with her, like before?

Eira says that's always a possibility. If it happens, though, it's a problem for Future Sam, not Today Sam. And also a problem for Future Eira and Future Dom. She says we'll deal with it together, if it happens.

She says, "Sam, you always have a choice. You can let what has happened crush you, or you can see it for what it is and use it to become stronger. Do you understand this?"

I think I do. I think it's also what Madame was talking about, finding your own voice. The voice of YOU. You have a choice about using that voice. Or staying silent.

I get an online video lesson with Madame now, once a month. Here's what she said during my lesson last week:

Remember this always. What you think, you are.

What you believe, you are.

But, most of all, what you do, you are.

And so, ma Cherie Sam, as I know you will, always think and believe and do your gift to the world. Because you are the only one who can.

The only one who can compose my music. Perform it. Or go to hear others perform it.

The only one who can give my special gift to the world.

To do that, I guess I better start liking airports.

Just like Umma tried to teach me.

the end

About the Author

Jacquelyn Johnson writes books for curious and creative kids ages 8 to 12.

She used to work as a newspaper and magazine writer and editor. Her articles and photographs have appeared in newspapers and magazines in Canada, United States and Britain.

Jacquelyn is also a former teacher, college and university lecturer. She has taught English as a Second Language to children and teenagers in South Korea and journalism to university students in South Dakota and Ontario.

When not writing, she enjoys watching her garden grow while doing as little actual garden work as possible, re-decorating her home with shabby chic finds (that means fixed up used stuff, a hobby she shares with Morley's mother, Eefa) and music.

She grew up studying piano and later played the trumpet, though regrets that she has never learned to play as well as Sam Park. Or make jewellery as well as Morley. Or ride horses, like Jayden can.

She makes her home and garden with her family near the ocean in a town very much like Seabright. Just down the street from a house that's very much like Morley's. With a little cat who's very much like Feather.

Acknowledgements

Thank you for reading Rules for Flying. I hope you've enjoyed your time with Sam and her friends.

Parenting is the most difficult job ever invented for amateurs. That said, I've known parents who, for a variety of reasons, just aren't as good at the job as they need to be. Many experts have helped in my understanding of such parents. Special thanks to Dr. Lindsay C. Gibson for her books of insights into both Soo Min's actions and Sam's: Understanding Emotionally Immature Parents and Adult Children of Emotionally Immature Parents.

I also gratefully acknowledge a BBC documentary that was immensely helpful in understanding why some women gamble to the point of addiction and why it is so difficult for them to stop.

Without the help and support of Wayne and Jesse, there would be no books completed, published and available to read. I am the most fortunate of writers to have such a loving family around me, supporting me as I write and helping to see that these stories reach you.

Seabright is not a copy of the town where I live, but a reflection of the many small, warm and welcoming towns and villages strung along the Atlantic coast of Northeastern United States and Canada's Maritimes.

acknowledgements

They are incredibly special places to live and work, write and play. I urge you to visit this peaceful and beautiful part of the world, if you ever get the chance. In the meantime, thanks for reading these stories that take place here, and perhaps dreaming of what your own life could be like in Seabright!

Lightning Source UK Ltd.
Milton Keynes UK
UKHW020205071020
371126UK00003B/217